Ben Ousman graduated in economics and was an executive at the Collège Saint-Laurent. He is the author of the novels *Vengeance en héritage tome 1, Plaisirs des misérables tome 1, Un Gay en cavale* published in French from Paris, France. He delivers his new novel *The Old Man and the Immigrants*.

I dedicate this novel to the immigrants who are fighting for the recognition of their qualifications and experiences in all fields in Canada. My hat is off to the old man, the tireless Daniel Sahel, who comforts the newcomers often in dramatic situations.

Ben Ousman

THE OLD MAN AND THE IMMIGRANTS

AUSTIN MACAULEY PUBLISHERS™

LONDON • CAMBRIDGE • NEW YORK • SHARJAH

Ordering Information
Quantity sales: Special discounts are available on quantity purchases by corporations, associations, and others. For details, contact the publisher at the address below.

Publisher's Cataloging-in-Publication data
Ousman, Ben
The Old Man and the Immigrants

ISBN 9781685623142 (Paperback)
ISBN 9781685623159 (ePub e-book)

Library of Congress Control Number: 2023906371

www.austinmacauley.com/us

First Published 2024
Austin Macauley Publishers LLC
40 Wall Street, 33rd Floor, Suite 3302
New York, NY 10005
USA

mail-usa@austinmacauley.com
+1 (646) 5125767

Chapter 1

The world has always been afraid of the word apocalypse. Some see it as a major upheaval that would put an end to earthly life, others believe they live it daily in endless conflicts that gnaw away at their lives, destroying their hopes. Everywhere, the earth burns, trembles, thunder rumbles. Lightning strikes blindly, destroying everything in their path. The natural calamity that has swept over humans passes, armed conflicts persist in every continent, throwing thousands of people out of their territories.

This apocalypse is the one experienced by refugees seeking a haven of peace.

Everywhere, they are in distress. In the Middle East, in Latin America, in Africa, in Asia as well as in the rest of the world. The ideological struggle crushes democracy, rehabilitates anarchy. The weapons speak, the executioners reign as kings and masters without empathy, there is danger everywhere. Massive executions of political opponents, blinding bombings killing more than millions of humans. There is neither food nor water; homes and hospital are destroyed. People running for their lives in others parts of the world, some arrive in Canada by plane, by boat, by crossing land borders, they tell the same horror stories.

Lodging in a hotel in Montreal, they start knowing other immigrants, they discover their new country.

Disorientated by the unknown environment, Amir could not believe that he could move freely through the streets of the city without skirmishes, without the dangers of the demarcation line dividing Beirut into two camps; he thought he was in another dimension. In his solitude inside this great haven of peace, he was surprised by the eagerness of the people in the morning and evening. Everything was running around him, but he heard neither the cannon fire nor the cries of the widows. The war was a thing of the past, he could not forget the mess he had found himself in.

At night, the difference of time with his country kept him awake; he was bored, he thought of his parents, his friends still caught in the traps of war. Suddenly, he heard a siren sound. What could it be? From his window, he saw the end of a race between the police and a fugitive. The patrol cars were barricading the street corners, policemen with guns on their wrists taking shooting positions, ordering the suspect to get out of his vehicle with hands up.

Amir panicked; he closed the window curtain halfway. The suspect fired several shots at the policemen, who unloaded their weapons on him. Slowly, they moved toward the car; one of them opened the door and shouted to his companions, "Call the ambulance!" The man lying on the seat was dead.

Amir was scared. Was it Beirut Two? He thought misfortune was upon him, even at several thousand kilometers from his native land. He thought he would be killed if he was outside. Disoriented, he became depressed again. He saw the executions that the belligerents carried out, like in a movie, when one neighbor denounced another. He saw the courage he had, braving the dangers of a besieged city over and over again. Without water or electricity, he lived with his family on the first floor of a building ruined by the relentless fire of the enemy's guns. They ate canned food bought on the black market; no one knew the city better than he did, having foiled the armed groups several times.

He went from one point to another in search of provisions. He remembered that one day, the sun had barely risen, and he went to the only bakery in the neighborhood that had not yet been destroyed. There was a long line of people waiting for bread. He waited for an hour and when it was his turn to buy some, an armed fighter came out of nowhere and fired into the air. Everybody lay down, he took the first place, serving himself and then disappeared. Tired, he finally fell asleep. When he woke up, he walked down by the few steps to the hotel cafeteria. A smiling waitress took his order and served him eggs that had just been turned on the stove. He pushed the smoked meat into a corner, fearing to eat the pork.

Shortly afterward, a young man of his age asked permission to sit at his table. He hesitated for a moment and then nodded his head. The waitress came back with three dishes in her hands, which Martinez swallowed in record time. He drank four cups of coffee, two cans of soft drink. On a full stomach, he unbuckled the belt of his greasy pants. "Would you like anything else, sir?" Asked the waitress as she cleared the table. Martinez looked around him, he gave the impression that he was asking the permission of the people in the restaurant before answering. Finally, he ended his breakfast with a hot chocolate.

Amir couldn't believe his eyes, what would he eat for lunch? At dinner? He imagined an army of dishes served at his table. "Where do you come from? From a concentration camp?" He asked his table companion. Martinez burst out laughing, how could he not recognize his gluttony? Indeed, it was due to the pressures that life exerted on him. It was his way of forgetting the war, drowning it in the dishes in order to better survive. Martinez replied in this term. "I am Salvadorian! I escaped the country for security reasons. It's hell in San-Salvador! Assassinations, kidnappings, the confrontation between the army and the guerrillas, I have to save my skin! It's not worth much in El Salvador."

Amir could not believe that a young person of his age had been subjected to the same living conditions in his country. Was it the curse? Why do human beings encourage bloodshed in order to achieve their political and economic ambitions? Breaking the established order, burning the earth. This land on which, once in power, he will try to water in a fleeting time, waiting for the defeated to return to conquest. This vicious circle seems to take the Third World into hostage, where democracy is moribund, amputated by the wrists of armed men who claim to be the liberators of the people.

With his hands in the face, his elbows on the table, Amir went further in his thinking, he hated those who decimated his family.

Amir and Martinez became friends, although they had lived through the war, they seemed to have come out of it matured by suffering. They were determined to be part of this new society. To rebuild their lives, to mop up the dark chapter of their lives. Guided by an old person, a patriarch. A man dedicated to the well-being of the newcomers, they headed for the neighborhood that immigrants called the United Nations. As the bus rolled along Park Avenue, they asked themselves, "How close is it to the United Nations?" The old man, a well-respected, smiled as they got off from the bus of the Montreal Urban Community, he said:

"Here, you are at the United Nations! A place of blessing where no one can feel any homesickness! Here, you are at home, everyone is Brother and Sister," exclaimed the old man. Daniel Sahel of his own name brought a smile on his face, he had just populated this venerated corner from where a large part of the nations of our planet lived together. A corner which according to his thought, excluded racial discrimination. With a rounded chest, he appeared as the baron of the place, smiling at all those who questioned him. He believed that he had been invested with a divine mission, that of helping the world in distress, the world similar to the one he had left to exile himself here, a promised land without a stain, it was said in his country before he came.

Visibly happy, the newcomers were surrounded by neighbors from the area. They wanted to know them, they wanted to know their country of origin, they especially wanted to know the political history that had thrown them on the streets. They did not have the idea that such a manifestation of joy hid a miserable life. They believed in true happiness when they saw the smiles on the faces of those people.

Daniel Sahel and some of his close friends took them to the apartment reserved for them. The wood steps were in extreme humidity, each step crushed. Inside, a ruin was discovered. Everything was left abandoned; an army of cockroaches had taken residence and lined the walls. The wooden floor creaked underfoot, old furniture housed mice, scurrying around, looking for new burrows. In the bathroom, the visibly rusty water pipe tried to make itself useful, the drop of water sounded like a military tambourine. The bowl filled with dried excrement had an unpleasant, breath-taking smell. In the rooms, graffiti replaced the curtains on the window, one could read the insults addressed to the negligent landlord who was afraid to face his tenants. Although small, they had the advantage of letting the neighbors' multiple languages, laughter, quarrels and communal meals be seen and heard.

The sun would finish its course toward sunset, the apartment had to be refreshed, cleaning and fighting the cockroaches. The beds had to be changed. Sheets, blankets. Daniel Sahel said, "You need help and it's in a hurry!" They presented themselves in front of a charity store. They took everything they needed-furniture and food.

Two Samaritans delivered the sets of living room, the companions carried the shopping. Suddenly, Martinez closed his eyes. He had a flash of his faraway run, in search of refuge; he saw the track he was taking, it always brought him back to the starting point. He was out of his mind; he didn't realize that he had just left this hell that was tracking him thousands of miles away. The last thing he wanted to review was the hostilities that decimated his family. He thought he was a great coward, unable to save his family. Hate overcame him, memories were still fresh in his mind.

Soon after, he regained the strength to carry his burden to the insalubrious, infested home.

At the beginning of December, the trees lost their leaves; the sun was setting earlier than usual. The temperature was dropping to unusual degrees, the companions watched people change their clothes. They were cold, they understood that they were no longer in the tropics. Soon after, the weather surprised them. A snowstorm hit Montreal and everything was buried in the streets. Motorists caught in the snow caused traffic jams, strong winds blew with the snow made visibility impossible. Broken trees tore down electrical wires, causing power outages and creating an apocalyptic atmosphere. Martinez thought he was at the North Pole; he had never experienced winter. He had the impression that after the massacres perpetuated by the guerrillas, nature was unleashed against him. Sitting on a chair, Amir had never encountered a climate as hostile as the war in Lebanon.

Then came the intense cold, running through the flesh to the bones. They shivered, teeth chattering. They didn't know that they had to turn on the heat. Amir couldn't take it anymore, he preferred the cannon fire, the sound of the machine-gun fire to the icy air that gave him no escape route. Suddenly, someone was knocking on the door. It was the janitor, his intuition made him go up to the new tenants' lodgings. They were frozen, they couldn't express themselves. The heating was turned on, half an hour later, they felt the heat. Their eyes glowed, they returned to the warmth they knew in their own countries. Little by little, they got rid of the heavy blankets, a kind of armor against this cold they had never known. They moved their fingers and toes. They got up; they made sure they could walk.

Ragged by this heat, Martinez had allowed himself an incursion on the balcony. He watched in amazement as the children threw snowballs at each other, rolling around on the floor, building men that they personified. He was thinking of his country; he saw a disaster. He thought that such snow shower would kill all the plantations, throw the population into famine. Discouraged, he folded his arms, he observed the gray sky lined with thick clouds, he could not detect any sunbeams. He worried at home that it was raining or thundering; the sky remained blue, the black clouds were synonymous with misfortune. Inside, they were short of provisions, it was out of the question to brave this unfriendly temperature. Either way, if they went in, they would get lost in the surrounding area.

The kind janitor came, helping them again with grocery; in a short time, he brought what they need and then he said: "You see! He said, I can offer you anything except women! I keep them to myself," followed by a burst of laughter. Amir took out of his pocket a bill of Lebanese currency and handed it to the concierge. "Is it enough to pay for the shopping?" He said. The concierge was surprised. "It's not worth a cent your money here! Welcome to the kingdom of the dollar! Go and clear your pockets!" Martinez gave him the amount he was asking for.

Four months later, the winter temperature gave way to spring. The sun melted the snow, the United Nations was awakening. We heard music here and there, we thought that the neighbors had given themselves the order to go out to celebrate.

In the building, music was disturbing Martinez. He put his ears against the wall, he wanted to listen to what was happening on the other side. He went out to the balcony, took a look around. Going down the stairs, then, he fell in the backyard. All the neighbors ran toward him, some yelling, others taking him into their homes. A mother surrounded by her children let him sleep on the sofa bed, and the eldest daughter applied compresses to him. She took a first-aid card out of her purse and pulled her mother aside.

Martinez had scratches on his knees and a small bump on his forehead. He seemed to have passed out deeply, Karen's soft hands woke him up as they walked over his body. He opened his eyes; he was astonished by the presence of all these people who were unknown to him. He couldn't remember how he had gotten to this house, people were smiling at him, he thought he was dreaming. He stared at Karen, he found her beautiful, elegant. She was the first to speak to him.

"What's your name?"

"Martinez!"

"I'm Karen, we have to go to the emergency! I don't know how your accident happened, what floor did you fall from?"

Martinez was silent, Karen whispered in his mother's ear, "Better let him rest, he looks better at home." While he was being pampered; Amir was looking for him everywhere. The old man of the United Nations phoned all the hospitals, Martinez remained untraceable. Yet he was in the apartment downstairs, six meters away. The next morning, two neighbors were chatting from their veranda about the rescued boy.

"Karen found herself a husband who had fallen from the sky!" The lady said rocking on her chair, the woolly threads between her legs, knitting a hood.

"Where did they come from? I haven't seen such a phenomenon for several years. Immigrants flying like butterflies, landing softly on the arms of women is wonderful for little Karen who has become an old maid, isn't it?" She recalled, gossiping, flipping through the pages of magazines.

Martinez was worried in turn, what would his friends say when they were barely found from the hotel? He felt bad, he asked permission to leave. Karen would like to keep him longer, she hesitated, then decided to accompany him to the apartment in front of the neighbors. It was quite a surprise, the old man was thinking of a passionate escape, when he saw the girl. Amir couldn't believe his eyes, gawking, he stared at Karen from head to toe. Basically, he would have acted the same way if something happened to him like his friend Martinez. "Take a seat, miss!" The old man shouted, while Martinez told how he had ended up at Karen's house. "Your story does not interest me," replied Amir, "you have the merit to go pick a rare flower in the middle of autumn, what great exploits?"

Martinez introduced her:

"Karen, this is my friend, Amir! This one is the old man of the neighborhood, you must have known him, he is nicknamed the old Negro."

"Don't listen to him! For some, I am the patriarch, the brain of the United Nations! Nice to meet you. Tell me, young girl, do your parents know you're here?"

"Yes, of course they do…They helped me take care of your friend."

"How nice."

He watched Karen from a distance, he didn't take his eyes off her until she came home. He wondered what to do to win the heart of such a beautiful girl. He thought back to the paths he had traveled to save his life from certain death. Now without a future, how could he please a girl? The old Negro saw him feeling guilty.

"You love her, don't you?"

"Yes, I do."

"Hurry up! You need a job! A girl like Karen is worth gold!"

The old Negro remembered his wedding in his home land in Africa; he offered ten cows, five oxen, fifteen sheep, forty chickens to marry the woman of his life. Martinez would be in trouble if such dowry was imposed to him. Fortunately for him, he was in Canada, there was no such tradition, the old Negro knew it. Finding work was a considerable challenge, the peers had understood this. They knocked on all the doors of the companies, they stormed the employment center, they sent hundreds of resumes. They had the strong conviction that one day the sun would rise with good news. Time went by, the work went away, the pile of mail they received said the same thing. It took Canadian experience to push a mop or broom through the mall corridors. Morals at the lowest level, they felt useless. But one day, they stopped at the neighborhood café, where they met an immigrant who had been living in Montreal for several years. Handsome in his outfit, the man was carrying a black briefcase that gave him great notoriety. He watched them for a long time, took his cup of coffee, and left to join them. Neither Amir nor Martinez thought he was a danger; a puzzle that would add to their hiring problem. The Third World mentality that remained in them suggested that such a person would be one to everything, and they were flattered.

"Hello, gentlemen. You seem to be fresh from elsewhere Ah!"

"We've only been here for a short time," Amir replied.

On the strength of what he had just heard, the man engaged in conversations touching on their sensitive points, he sold his salad without dressing.

"Do you like it here?"

"It's paradise on earth!" Amir replied.

"I see, you're not homesick. All immigrants like the United Nations when they arrive, they leave with difficulty."

It was the first time that someone other than the old man was interested in them. They listened to him religiously, the man of providence, and he offered to help them get a job. He pretended to be a doctor treating businessmen, ready to use his influence to get them jobs. The companions had to pay a small sum for the formality. Two hundred and fifty dollars is not a lot of money for positions in their field. The man offered them a meal and paid the bill. This kindness gave confidence to the companions; they were in a hurry to pay the sum requested.

"Here are two hundred and fifty dollars, we are eager to work."

The man's hands were shaking, he stared them in the eyes and then he restrained himself. Martinez added:

"In my country, one pays a thousand times what the heads of companies ask for here!"

"No! You will hand-deliver it to them. You know, I suffered before I managed to place myself as a doctor, what a bad memory every time I see immigrants in this situation."

He edited a false emotion, wiping his eyes without tears. The story of his suffering, his perseverance, blinded his companions. The next day, they met him at the café accompanied by a man with a red briefcase in his hand. Could this be the sign of danger? They did not know, all that mattered was the posts in their domain. They were somehow hypnotized, they were fixated. They believed in the miracle, they let themselves be led unsuspectingly down a dead-end road, toward abandonment. The interview was short, they filled out forms and then paid the fees. They were given business cards, a kind of bogus guarantee that transformed their lives in record time, lifting them above the hierarchy. It was total euphoria, an immense joy that made them forget who they were, where they came from. They jumped up, shouted their joy. If they could, they would stop time, they would announce the news to the whole city and the suburbs that they were getting the dividend of perseverance. They were already thinking about which subway to take, in which direction should they go? They had to start work in a week.

Martinez announced the news to the old man, he deserved the exclusivity because of his kindness toward them, his availability to help them, to deal with all the good or bad subjects. Daniel Sahel was breathless, he could not have believed his ears, he was certain that he would not have heard everything. When he knew the truth, he went to hold them close to him, this double success could not go unnoticed, good news was rare in the United Nations. He underlined this feat worthy of fiction with a big party. Among the guests, many were unemployed, bottle of beer in hand, they paraded in front of the comrades, sifting them with questions. The first tall man, with a swarthy complexion, spoke loudly, spittle came out of his mouth and monopolized the conversation. He drank from the bottle, took a big sip of half of the contents and then went to get another one and opened it, his steel teeth replaced the traditional bottle opener. Sitting on a stool in front of the kitchen, he addressed Martinez.

"Tell me, kid, how do you manage to get good jobs in such a short time? Look around you, all these beautiful people had ambitions equal to yours, they had self-esteem by treading the ground head high, they were convinced that they would have a better life to the point of swimming in wealth. They thought that one day they would return to their countries with their hands full of money. They were given the rare welcome reserved for heads of state. Red carpet rolled out, a guard of honor, men and women prostrated before them, claiming their share of the cake. Isn't it a beautiful dream, my little one? Look what we have become! Parasites! Yes, society has made us marginalized, voiceless men, while keeping us for life with little jackpot to say that we exist!"

A second nicknamed Diallo was walking staggering around, lost his glasses, he bumped into the wall, the old man made him sit by the window, he commented on the day's event. He shouted at anyone who wanted to hear him.

"Listen to me! Boys, you make lie the legend that if you enter into the ghetto, all the doors will be closed to you."

Not far away, a man with sad looks had both hands on his head. He was dreaming of the day when luck would smile on him. He had lost hope for several years, the failure of his efforts had led him into deep depression. The man's hand was shaking, one of his feet was shaking tirelessly, giving the impression of being in agony. He seemed to be calling for death in order to free him from the social burden, the pressure he was under, the repeated failure in his attempts to lead a normal life, he would have been unable to see himself idle, destitute, unable to provide honorably for his basic needs. Suddenly, his tears flowed, he got up from his chair, kneeling on the floor, with his hands stretched out to the sky he cried out in anger.

"Oh my God! Tell me when…please tell me when…would I become useful? Look at me! Don't turn away from me! Make me happy or take me into your kingdom! I beg you. I can't take it anymore! I can't take it anymore!"

The man fainted; the ambulance came to pick him up in front of his comrades. What sad life? What tragedy? It would have been useful to society that fed him to the small amount of the last public by offering him a chance to recognize his diplomas, to hire him, to train him without restriction, to make him a tax-paying citizen, a full-fledged citizen, a citizen at all. The last person who asked to speak changed his mind, preferring to remain silent. Deep down, he was ashamed of his exit, while wondering inwardly how to get out of this infamous life, in order to lead a rich, happy life. All he dreamed of was this very distant fulfillment, which seemed so close when he saw the success of these young men. This internal struggle that he undertook against himself gnawed at his mental balance, the vicious circle came back to haunt him more and more beautifully, he saw rising before him a mountain of difficulties that could stem his future projects, he shivered from head to toe. When he came back to himself, he said with a slow voice, barely able to express himself. He wanted to congratulate them, to take off his hat in front of such an unequivocal professional breakthrough.

"You are angels, blessed children of God. I wish you all the best in your new professional careers."

A flashbulb opened in his memory, he found himself in his native country. The dictator Sékou Touré had decimated his family. His father executed; the presidential guard was looking for him.

Returning from a soccer match, Diallo was intercepted by a neighbor a few yards from the family home, he was reliving those sad moments.

"Boy! Stop, I have bad news for you, the presidential guard is looking for you."

"Why are they looking for me? What had I done?"

"Stop exposing yourself, come to my house."

"Are you joking or what? No one can stop me; I am the son of a government minister."

"Disillusion yourself! Your father is no longer there, armed soldiers are in front of the house, waiting for family members."

Diallo followed the man inside; his heart was beating so fast that he thought he was dying. With his breaths cut off, he urged the man to tell him the truth.

"What happened to my father?"

"The soldiers executed him!"

"My mother, my sisters?"

"They were executed."

"No! Let me out, I'll go to them!"

"They are waiting for this; they will kill you!"

Diallo fought with all his strength against his savior, he hit him. The man and his wife overpowered him, they tied him to a chair. Diallo knew that politicians' children were victims of kidnapping, he shouted at the top of his voice.

"Help! Help! Help! I'm being held hostage! I'm Diallo, free me, do something, talk to my father!"

"Shut up, you little idiot, we're saving your life!" Cissé said.

The couple closed his mouth with a blindfold, Diallo took his eyes out of his sockets, no one could hear him. Suddenly, the national television was singing the national song, then letting the dictator appear on the screen. He made a speech to the nation, talking about an abortive coup d'état, Camara's name came up in every word, Diallo couldn't believe his ears. Everywhere the soldiers were looking for him, Cissé locked him in a closet when someone knocked on his door.

"Have you seen the little Diallo?" They asked.

"No, we don't know him!"

"Liars! You know him well. You were at the many parties he organized in his villa house."

"You are mistaken about me."

"We will search the house, but keep in mind that if we find him here, you will be executed on the spot!"

"Make yourselves at home, valiant soldiers."

They searched the house with a fine-toothed comb, Diallo trembled with all his soul, the soldiers took their time. One of them standing in front of the closet, they would go through the interrogations. Cissé's residence was only a few meters away from Camara's residence.

"Your name!"

"Cissé."

"The name of your father!"

"Konaté."

"Your mother?"

"Aminatou."

"Where do they live?"

"Conakry."

"Well, Cissé Konaté. You will tell me the whole truth about your neighbor, Camara, the push does not prepare itself, your life, that of your whole family depends on what will come out of your mouth."

"I know nothing of what you say."

"Well, we'll see about that."

He called out to his men who were still in the vehicle, they came in pointing their guns at the couple, they waited for the captain's order.

"Soldiers! Make them talk."

Cissé and his wife were beaten with sticks, they were beaten to death. Crouching on the floor, they could not free the young Diallo from the closet, they spent the night in pain. In the morning, an aunt came in and found them among the ransacked furniture.

"Cissé! Fatimatou! Oh, my God, the assassin has already passed through here. May God curse the devil Sékou Touré, may he carry his soul to hell!"

She lifted them up, their faces stained with clotted blood. Cissé crawled toward the cupboard, beckoned to Fatimatou to open it. As soon as she did, Diallo fell to the floor, he lost consciousness. The soldiers had not found anything abnormal; they would not return after stealing the jewelry, clothing, or even imported objects. Everywhere in the streets, the presence of military was imposing, they would point their weapons at whomever they suspected. Cissé almost died, he decided to take refuge in the neighboring country.

"Listen, my little one, you saw the danger with your own eyes, you heard me screaming under the blows of the truncheons. Look at my wounds, I can't go to the clinic, my older sister is a nurse and she will come to help us."

"Thank you, Mr Cissé, I owe you, my life."

"Your parents were good people; they helped the whole neighborhood. They freed prisoners who were victims of tribal discrimination, I would protect you with my life."

"What are we going to do now? We are prisoners in this house."

"You will come with us to the refugee camps in neighboring countries, here, our life is worthless."

Diallo came out of his ordeal to face the present again, he remained silent while he recovered from his emotions. All this was in the past, an unforgettable past that haunted Cissé, disturbed his sleep. He thought he had found tranquility in Canada, a carefree life that would make him forget the nightmares. He realized that it wasn't all over, another fierce battle awaited him. That of his profession, doctor, his diploma was not recognized, he could not even hold the position of nurse. As a cab driver, he could not pay his rent, could not eat properly. He didn't know where to put his head, he often looked at himself in the mirror, he cried in his small apartment, a room that looked like a prison cell. He no longer existed; his life was reduced to nothing. The encouragement of the old Negro made him wipe away the tears, he was at the same time their psychologist, their psychiatrist. A wise patriarch who did not mince his words, who denounced the racism suffered by immigrants of all nationalities. Tireless, he succeeded in making them smile in dramatic moments. He made them keep hope, he prayed, he said that one day the favorable winds would blow in their direction. The man was waiting for his salvation, he listened to him religiously, he asked him:

"When will this happen? I am drowning in extreme poverty. I do eat bread and jam. The only luxury I allowed myself was when I went to beg, to ask permission to rummage through the butcher's junk containers for fat and bones at the Jean-Talon market."

Daniel Sahel looked him in the eyes, he answered.

"The United Nations where we live is nothing but a large refugee camp, no one is interested in our fate. They only come to get us to fill in the holes, dirty holes that they refuse to dirty their hands. My brave boy, keep hope, little by little the bird is settling down and making its nest. I am not a seer, be strong, persevere, one day life will smile on you."

Two weeks passed, the news from the hospital had not been good. In the middle of watching satellite soccer games in a neighborhood bar, Daniel Sahel entered with his head down, dragging his feet as if he had just come back from a funeral. He caught everyone's attention and then told them the irreparable.

"Listen friends! Please, listen to me!"

He could hardly speak, his tears flowed like a stream, his voice trembling he announced the death of the one who could no longer bear his living conditions. There was a long silence, the Muslims said may God had his soul, the Christians exchanged the cross.

The death of Michel Louvain did not prevent the hardcore members of the party from organizing an evening of felicity, in fact, a way to encourage the companions in their future tasks. Daniel Sahel promulgated his wise man's advice. "Listen to me!" he shouted to the youth. "It is of paramount importance to do your job well, be punctual! Follow the instructions of your superiors. Produce more than what is required, go last to the coffee break, get up first for work. Don't forget! It's quantity and quality that will get you there." Motionless on the chair, Martinez nodded, every word he said, so long as Amir found the time long. Obviously, he seemed to be tired of hearing the same speech over and over again. He played feverishly with the debris of the chicken bones and the empty skim milk carton piled up in the tray in the middle of the table.

Although he was bothered by the smoke from his interlocutor's pipe, Martinez was worried about the burden that awaited him. The uncertainty of the role he would have to play in his duties made him see an immense desert to cross, the idea of facing this unfamiliar world sucked up all his energies. Will he really succeed in this career? He who knew nothing other than to advise the farmers how to stir up the land? Daniel Sahel emptied his bottle, nodded from afar, commanding a big one. He was looking for words to console his young friend, he ended up saying: "My, little one! Don't worry, both of you have potential! Don't compare yourself to me, old Negro who is just waiting for death to come and give him the final blow."

Daniel Sahel had a big heart; he took a handkerchief out of his pocket and wiped his tears. These tears that he shed with each negative mail to his thousands of job applications, would form a backwater, or even a lake if he collected them. His eyes reddened with emotion; he was lost. He no longer knew who he was, where he was.

"Is everything alright?" Martinez cried. Slowly, he brought him back to the present.

"Forgive me, my brave boy, I was in another world, the world of the afflicted fills with sadness. Thank God, your presence gave me hope."

The old man's behavior gave Martinez goosebumps. In him, a patriarch was the essence of wisdom, a person whose knowledge went beyond borders. He no longer knew what ship he was getting into.

The party was in full swing, the music was playing throughout the building. Inconvenienced, the neighbors rang the doorbell. The most soulful of the guests showed up and asked:

"What do you want?"

"Turn down your stereo! We can't sleep!"

He heard a lady holding her newborn baby in her hand. The man burst out laughing, a laugh that shocked the neighbors. They insisted, the man bounced back:

"Sleep? It's Saturday today! Come on! Come in the whole gang, dance with us, we are celebrating the success of two friends!"

The lady's face was reddened with anger.

"Don't you want to understand anything? I have a child who can't sleep! It's late to play music in the building, turn it down!"

The response she received was disappointing, quickly the gap between the partygoer and the neighbors widened.

"Yes! Yes! I don't understand why a beautiful woman like you spends her time sleeping? Listen, today is Saturday night fever. Either you go dancing or you go home without playing the party troublemaker!"

The neighbors were getting angry, diplomacy gave way to escalation. Everyone was giving his opinion, one of them angry and came forward with a rounded chest, spitting in the doorman's face, throwing oil on the fire. Martinez had arrived, the conditions were right for a fight to break out. They showed the third finger to whoever wanted to see, they threw insults on both sides without respect. The most audacious made their way for better being heard, he monopolized the word, then dropped a bomb. The bomb was sounded all the way inside the house, and the guests had left when they heard one of the complainants say:

"Since you have invaded this neighborhood, we have no peace and quiet! This peaceful place has been transformed into a hell of a place, it's worse here than in Harlem!"

This word sounded the death knell, awakened the conscience of those who knew the history of racism in the United States. They felt attacked, scorned because of their culture, their difference, their way of life, their way of being. In a jumble, they let off steam, they looked for the most hurtful words to bring down their opponent.

"Ha, ha! Harlem, you say? It's beautiful there! We are finally going to liven up this ugly neighborhood where everything is asleep! Do not blame us if you are unable to offer you an evening party, we are well at home, do not stop us from living."

Another obviously drunk partygoer dropped his missile before vomiting in front of the door, the smell made the gathering of the disgruntled retreat.

"Listen to me! If you are unhappy! If you feel like a minority in the United Nations! If you are not worthy to live next to us! You have only one choice, leave the area, go somewhere else! Yes, leave the United Nations!"

The third one took his head out of the door, he added:

"But one day...we'll join you; you wouldn't know where to put your head! Ha! Ha! Ha! Ha! I swear by my grandfather's beard! We will join you! Whether you're in Laval or Longueil, we'll be there! You would have no choice but to endure us...unless you decide to give birth to more children...I doubt it! You love freedom too much to take care of children! You would see us arrive in large numbers, like the St Lawrence River flowing toward the sea."

"Is that enough to roll up your arms? Show your teeth? It would be simple to turn down the music, to listen, to understand others, to be tolerant, to open up more so as not to fall into the traps of racism," words that could put the powder on the fire. From a distance, coming patrol car, it was buzzing from both sides when the cops came down, when they asked:

"Is this where the noises are?" Asked one of the cops.

"Yes! Evict those imported! They're poisoning our lives!" Shouted the most talkative.

"Gentlemen! Calm down, answer my question, are you the ones who called us?"

"Yes! They break our eardrums with their music, we can't sleep or watch the hockey game. It's Saturday, we need to rest, damn tell them!"

The policemen met the party people, Martinez asked the cops what volume they were entitled to. He put the music back to the threshold volume. Outside, the intolerance raised the crowd at the cops' exit.

"You didn't do anything in there!" Said a man. "You're worse than those immigrants!"

"Watch your language! The music is low."

"Are you sick? They'll turn it up when you leave! It's the world upside down, I'm a native from here, I'm losing my right at the expense of these vultures coming from overseas. No! I won't stop there! You will hear me speak; you will repent! We would go and destroy these musical instruments! You would come back in the middle of a racial scandal!"

Martinez calmed down his neighbors, he put an end to the evening. They were leaving the apartment for a nightclub. Daniel Sahel introduced them to his old friends who had come to join them at the table.

"They are our heroes! They have just landed jobs."

"Really?" One of them exclaimed. "We have to celebrate! With the big paychecks, no more rarity for us, you'd think of your old people, they won't have empty bottles at the table anymore."

The names circulating in the bar were Martinez, Amir. Everybody came to their table, each one told his past, his experience. Among all these people, Adyenn distinguished himself by his frank speech:

"Tell me, kids! How do you manage to get jobs in record time? It's magic! Since my arrival, I have been living only on social assistance, tell me your secret so that I can get out of this miserable life."

"It's because they are more intelligent than us, they don't wait for a job falling from the sky. There aren't three like them who could get out of the shit."

This last intervention provoked the anger of Adyenn, he felt insulted. He waited several years for the position he coveted to fall from the sky. To call him unintelligent was to murder him, to take away all hope, to ruin the perseverance that kept him in balance while waiting for the beautiful day. He had a devastating reply.

"Who are you to mock me? Just suck your bottle. I'd be the prime minister of Canada if it wasn't the color of my skin! I'm more intelligent than those who govern. Here you go! Here! I'll prove it to you."

"Can you hear the alcohol talking? He thinks he's the prime minister of the Banana Republic! Brother, you have to be white to rule Canada! With this black skin, you'll clean the seats of parliament in Ottawa. Ha! Ha! Ha!"

"Shut up! You don't know me! You underestimate me! On the contrary, I reset the clock. Wake up, stop your crazy dream that is leading you adrift."

The old Negro put an end to this argument, he was rather preoccupied with where his boyfriends will be living. Few people with such positions live in the United Nations; they should stay there, it would be necessary that they remain there to moralize their old and young friends, women, men, children thirsting for success in this world different from theirs, this world they saw it getting further and further away, they saw it passing like the train difficult to catch up with, difficult to take a seat on board.

Chapter 2

The days passed. Martinez waited in vain for the phone call. Locked up in the apartment, the two friends could not imagine that it was a trick. Every time the phone rang, they were full of hope, it was the friends of the United Nations, they kept on congratulating them. The sun setting on the horizon, Martinez made the cross on the promised posts, while Amir was still hopeful. He thought he had not clearly indicated the telephone number. They were content with the idea without closing their eyes all night. In the morning, they called the number on the business card. A recorded message announced that there was no service at the numbers they dialed. It was a disaster, consternation; they went to the address on the card and found themselves at the charity building. Martinez opened the door; he saw in front of him beds lined up from which several people were lying down. With the business card in his hand, he shouted the name of the guy relentlessly. A strong man came to meet them.

"Shut up! It's a place of rest here!"

"So, you are sheltering the robbers, if you don't give us the holder of this card, there will be a police raid in your lodge!"

The tension was rising, suddenly, the man lost his patience. He advanced dangerously toward Martinez, he intended to fight.

"Ah! No joke, it's because of you that we are living in this shit house! The government is congested by your problems here and elsewhere! Look at the clothes you're wearing, I can't even afford them, yet my whole generation of family was tax payers. Get out immediately, dirty immigrants!"

They were trying to ease their suffering, what could they say to all these people, who kept quoting them as an example? They were mentally torturing themselves in the face of this humiliation, this bitter defeat. It was obvious that these poor brave young men had been victims of the scams. The will to succeed took over the caution. What a horror to think of ending one day around like vagabonds, joining the ranks of those who wake up every morning in the torment of life with no way out. They took Atwater Street; they improvised how to get out of the shame, the humiliation after they had raised so much hope at the United Nations. If they could, they would disappear from traffic, they would go to an unknown place, to digest their setback. In short, another sanctuary that would welcome them, that could offer them a place of refuge, condition them, shape them like clay, emerge in a mold with a new body, a face different from the known ones.

Where would they find this place? Who would lead them there? Who would wipe away their tears and ease their pain? How would they find themselves once this devastating pain will be over? How would they find themselves once this social crisis known by several peoples will pass away?

Dreamers on the road of disgrace, they avoided the people of the neighborhood; they went out early, came home late. The only refuge they had was a shopping mall far from the residence. They liked it; they could once again reconnect with their utopian dreams. After all, they didn't have to pay a fee for window-shopping. They believed that all the stores belonged to one person. Going from department to department, they choose a few items, they didn't know they were leaving the store. Soon, a man walked their way, then he asked them to follow him.

"Who are you?"

"Store security, you have committed an infraction."

"We are not criminals," Martinez defended himself, "we are new to the country."

"Did you pay for the goods in your possession?"

"No!"

"Then you stole."

"We are still in the mall!"

"But not in the store!"

"We are honest people, sir!"

The security guard had no forgiveness despite the innocence on their faces. He had just proved to his superiors that he was efficient; no marauder could escape him. Smiling broadly to his ears, he put on more of his own.

"All immigrants are thieves, if you don't steal the jobs, it's the goods you steal. The prisons in your countries are full, you are probably the ones who escaped, but here I have you in my grasp!"

They didn't know what to do; after the crooks, they became criminals. They waited for hours in a small room full of boxes, locked. When the door opened, they were policemen. One of the officers was questioning them, Martinez told how he thought all these businesses belonged to one person. The sincerity appeared in their faces, and they were released immediately.

Martinez told his friend that they were in the land of justice, in El Salvador, as soon as you were suspected of theft, the police beat you to the point of blood, forcing you to confess to the crime you did not commit. They had had too much for one day, disgusted, they would go home, thinking of their injury. They didn't feel like talking about work anymore, but a few minutes later, there was a knock on their door. Who could it be? Yet they made sure that their trip was discreet. They looked at each other and then silence reigned in the house. Curiosity to know who was in the door led Amir walking on tiptoes, his nose stuck to the window, he glanced outside. When he saw the old man, he ran to open the door. Looking down, it was easy to notice that they were hiding something. Leaning on his cane, the old Negro turned on the living room light. Well seated on the couch, he cleaned his pipe which he held preciously by hand and then made his comments.

"It's tiring the beginning of a career, don't give up!"

The companions remained silent for a moment, it seemed as if they lost their tongues. They wondered whether they should laugh or cry. Bitterness overwhelmed them, disappointment, fear of facing those who saw in them extraordinary geniuses made them shed tears.

"Daniel, we didn't get the jobs." Answered Martinez shyly.

Hard to believe, the old Negro took it as a joke. He was going back and forth in front of the door without seeing them, he took it for nonsense, he persisted.

"You are kidding me! Where were you then?"

The adventure they had was painful to recount in detail, without any after-effects. But they had to get out of it, turn the page on the torment of their setbacks, manage to keep their morals. Martinez had a little smile on his face, he sat down in front of the old man.

"I am sincere!" he repeated, "we were victims of a scam."

The Dean dropped his pipe, he got up abruptly, paced, he emptied his heart. It is inconceivable that these young people full of good will should be reduced in the same way as those who had gone before them. The old memories of the better living conditions he had come to find were coming back, he would like them to get out of it. But this carapace, this title that designates a race coming from elsewhere, this disturbing word 'immigrant' was a major handicap, a stain that sticks to the skin, an image that frightens the ignorant, even some intellectuals. Constantly nodding his head, it was his turn to let his emotions out: "It's difficult to carve out a respectable place for oneself in this society. It's hard to find a respectable place for ourselves in this society," he said. "We endure the failures in our attempts to raise our heads, to work, to live decently, inactivity is eating away at our health. It pushes some of us into depression, others into a dead-end path of social assistance, a career that is offered to us by treading the ground." He thought of his capricious young nephew, a local boy who believed he had conquered the hearts of all those he came into contact with, must have had both feet on the ground. He shivered, he put his coat back on. The sorrow, the regret of not being what he was in his native country, the lies he told his friends in his letters made him shed tears.

He was a pious man, respected, he was the one who intervened to make justice reign, he was unemployed with no future trying to regain his balance. But the story of the companions caught up with his own.

Returning to his home, he had a note to call his little sister back. She organized a birthday party at his place. The old man was not in the mood to celebrate his birthday despite his thousand arguments, his sister wanted to do so. She took care of all the food, the drinks, she bought little treats that the old man could not afford. On Friday evening, Annie surprised her son Abraham who had not seen his uncle for two months. As he used to do, as soon as he returned from school, Abraham asked the eternal question:

"What are we going to do tonight, Mom?"

"We will go to the United Nations. By the way, your uncle is celebrating his birthday today. I've organized everything, there will be guests. The only favor I'm asking you is to be polite to the guests."

Abraham gave a high-pitched cry; he would accept anything except to go to a place he called a ghetto.

"There is no way I am going there!"

"Yes, you will come!"

"No! I don't want to make a fool of myself, they speak badly of me I won't go and shame you."

"Don't reject your own people, be proud of where you come from. Immigrants do not have an easy life in this country."

"Do they integrate? It will only help them."

"Integration does not mean assimilation; I point out that a child without customs is a tree without roots."

"You have assimilated their bullshit well!"

The taxi was in front of the door, Abraham took a long time to go down the few stairs leading to the car. On the way, the taximan commented on each street he crossed, he said: "This neighborhood was once inhabited by pure wool Quebecers; today, we no longer find each other, immigrants of all nationalities live there. Every time I go in, I feel disorientated, here they live like in the Third World, they have made their countries in miniature."

Annie pulled out her hinges while Abraham had broad smiles on his face. She felt she was being targeted; she took it as a provocation.

"Sir! Mister! We, we are Quebecers of what category? You dream of a pure race in this century, what utopia?"

The neighborhood belongs to everyone, no one chased you away.

The old man's apartment was invaded by his friends, it was the first time Martinez faced a UN crowd. The old man had planned everything, talked about everything except the work of his friends. Eyes turned to Abraham, everyone wanted to say a word to him: "Abraham, you have grown up, Abraham, we did not recognize you." Sitting next to a drunk man, he was under constant interrogation. Abraham pretended to read the book he was holding in his hand. Dissatisfied, the man approached him, the support of his chair served as a support. Suddenly, he fell onto a tray filled with hors d'oeuvres on a bench waiting to be served. His clothes were stained with oil, so he went to get a stool to chat.

"Do you know me?"

"No, I don't know you!"

"I am your uncle's best friend."

"What the hell!"

"The last time I saw you, you were only ten years old."

"Where were you? In jail?"

"No! No! Kid, don't talk nonsense!"

Abraham got up in turn and locked himself in the bathroom. When he came out, the old man introduced him to Martinez and Amir: "I think you're going to get along with this one. He doesn't live in our neighborhood, he's the rebel of the family. Every time he sees me, he reproaches me. Today, he's holding back for my birthday. From tomorrow, he's going to call me idle even though he knows that at my age, I will never be able to find a job. He knew that in my country I was a high-ranking civil servant. Everything was at my disposal. Women, money, materials. I don't accept that those who bowed down to me for favors can say that my life is a fiasco. To show up, I was standing in front of beautiful cars, beautiful luxury properties. I took pictures and sent them to my friends at my home land, let them see how I am rich here in Canada. But God knows that I was lying."

Martinez who knew too much about the powers in his country consoled him. "In these countries," he said, "everything is ephemeral. Coup d'état here and there, they confiscate the property of some, and deprive others of their freedom. You left your country in honor; others had done so in dishonor."

The Dean was delighted to see the self-esteem of his companions rise through his past; they were the only ones to speak such language. Usually, he would get caught by his old friends in interminable conversations about the politics of the countries they had left.

On Sunday afternoon, the sun continued to shine, the sky was blue without clouds, the temperature reached twenty degrees Celsius. Abraham walked for the first time in the company of his uncle, Martinez and Amir. He was their guide, leading them to Mount Royal Park. A magnificent, very lively place that the Dean was unaware of its existence. They rushed to the chalet where they learned about the history of Montreal. Inside, the Dean thought of the founder. "He has the merit of having created a marvel at the foot of this gigantic mountain." He admired the skyscrapers from above. He would like to be one of the first tireless pioneers who made the city what it is today. He believed that providence was not there when he was conceived far from this place from which he would have to spend the rest of his days. Pushed on their backs by Abraham, they stormed into Beaver Lake. Each one rented his pelican pedal boat, they went there and back, running. Tired, they let themselves float in the middle.

"Where is the river that feeds this lake?" Asked Martinez.

"There is no river!" Shouted Abraham.

"But where does the water come from?" He persisted.

"It is an artificial lake. We are now circulating on the crater of an extinct volcano!"

Scared, he already saw the devastation of an erupting volcano. Who could assure him that the city would not be set on fire? Save who can, he went out at high speed, pedaling with all his strength. Laughter and laughter, his friends went crazy. Little by little, they were going to give their boats back. Martinez felt good with both feet on the ground, he no longer had his breath taken away. Dinner time came quickly, even though the sun hadn't yet set, it was eight o'clock. The bus that was supposed to bring them home was late; they decided to eat at the cottage. It was sandwiches, the Dean, the Negro man didn't understand that people love this dish as if there was nothing else in the gastronomy. He pushed away the aluminum foil and everything in it. Abraham glanced at the companions and burst out laughing. "My uncle," he said, "integration in North America begins with hot dogs, poutine and hamburgers." The Dean kept rinsing his mouth, he spat and spat back into the garbage can. He thought back to his favorite dish prepared by his servants in Africa, he felt guilty, regretting having lost all these privileges. He felt that he had made the decision to immigrate to Canada without realizing the consequences. Dreaming over Mount Royal, he let himself be teased by Abraham.

"Many immigrants," he said, "are not happy anywhere. They get nostalgic when they face the slightest obstacle. Suddenly, the country they had fled became the best place to live. It didn't take long to reject outright what they had come here to Canada to seek. My friends' parents had gone back to their homeland and sold all their property. A year later, they were back. The mentality of the people in their country was no longer the same as they had known."

The Dean couldn't believe his ears, it would have been difficult for him to step on his pride and the way, to go and be laughed at? What a double failure! He grumbled, he grumbled. But he had admiration for this tenacious young boy, who didn't mince his words even if everything he said hurt him deeply.

His words sounded like a bomb among his friends. They saw themselves trapped, they who had just arrived would do without such an example.

"If I understood correctly, their skills were not recognized. They were noble people, they went back to the nobility, but there they came up against the change that took away their crown? I did well to endure my professional defeat in intimacy." Cherishing the Dean. No sooner had he finished his word that he got his nephew's line.

"You didn't do anything, uncle, I'm young and I deliver newspapers!"

"If I understand correctly, you're blaming me for not making enough effort! To go for it," he said, "you have to know the environment. How would the newcomer, who barely knows his home, do it? The information we were given upon arrival did not allow any immigrant to integrate. That's why, desperate, we gathered in the same neighborhood to fight against boredom, disorientation, culture shock!"

Martinez asked for clarification on the shortcomings he experienced during his attempts to get out of work. According to him, the Dean, the old Negro would be the best person to inform him.

"What is the Canadian experience? Everyone is talking about it."

"It's the business visa, after the immigration visa. If you don't have this visa, you'll be going around in circles for the rest of your life."

"You have to add to this bilingualism," Martinez continued.

"Don't worry!" cried the Dean, "with multiculturalism, we wouldn't need to be bilingual anymore. We would soon be served in Italian, Arabic, Portuguese and even in African patois, what's the problem?"

These sentences made Abraham blush, he who had never been treated as a native, a pure wool Quebecer as the taximan had hinted to his mother, he exploded.

"Are you sick, uncle? Two cultures can't manage to cohabit, we would have to add others?"

"That's what Canada is all about! Find out more! My little one."

"Those who think like that should pack their bags!"

Sunday's conversations had no influence on Martinez; from Monday morning, he returned with his friend to the employment center, they were determined to do any job. On Wednesday afternoon, the phone rang. Amir picked up the line.

"Hello!"

"Martinez or Amir please!"

"Amir listening!"

"Michel from the agricultural employment center, are you still interested in working?"

"Of course, sir! What good news."

"Take note, go to this address for an interview."

"Thank you, sir! We will be there."

The bad experience they had had somehow prevented them from spreading the news this time. They didn't know what position they were interviewing for; they were mentally torturing themselves along the way. They took a cab about fifty kilometers out of town, the car headed for Rougemont. There were apple trees as far as the eye could see along the road, loaded with apples. The smell of the farm brought Martinez back to his native country. Finally, he recognized himself in these fields, which were very different from his own, what can they say about this breathtaking landscape. They remained amazed when they set foot on the ground. A man of small stature and not very talkative was waiting for them in a hut among the apple trees. The man motioned for them to sit down and then began the interviews even to pick the apples. They were lost, they didn't know what to say.

"Who sent you here?"

"The employment center, sir!"

"Do you have experience?"

"No, sir! But we are able to do any job you would give us."

The man was staring at them, he always looked angry. He kept a moment of silence and then he bounced back as if he felt insulted to have them in front of him. He had nothing against the immigrants, but he had a kind of surprise, a culture shock. For several years, when apple picking season came, there were only Quebecers from the stumps who came to work or immigrants who were called non-visible when all the colors are visible. The words stem and visible are not unanimous, many consider that they create three categories of citizens of which those most discriminated are the ones called visible as if the two others cannot be seen with the naked eye. The man behaved like an employer requiring knowledge and experience in the field.

"That's it! They always send us people who have never picked apples! Are you able to empty an apple tree? I mean to empty the entire tree of its load of apples."

A coldness seized Martinez and his friend; they had this fear of doing a job under pressure from a strict boss who would have an eye for the slightest detail. Fearing that they would not learn this fruit-picking trade well created a climate of panic in their minds. They would quickly come out of their dreams to answer to the apple boss.

"Yes, sir!"

"Well, you see these baskets? Filled with apples give you fifty cents each."

Martinez was expecting hourly rates, he was surprised at the mode of remuneration based on the unit of the basket filled with apples. They were thinking, they told each other that the experience of picking would help them in their search for other jobs outside the countryside.

Perched on the stepladder, they picked several apples at a time, without taking into account the picking technique as taught to them by a young man next to them. The owner shouted from afar, he was at the end of his nerves. He saw his precious treasures falling from all sides of the apple trees, his hair stood up, he blushed with anger, he got out of his damn tractor pulling a long wagon that was used as a picker's depot. If he could, he would tear off their heads for every apple that was badly picked, which could reduce his income. Walking with giant steps, he shouted from afar, preferring not to strangle one.

"Hey! You, there! I don't know what jungle you come from; apples are like eggs! If that doesn't suit you, get out!"

He once showed them the best method of picking: "Look here," he said, "you grab one and turn it gently, without scratching it or it loses its market value."

This method would not allow the companions to fill the baskets quickly. Nevertheless, they were determined to finish the day at the farm. At sunset, they managed to accumulate together the sum of twenty-five dollars.

Happy with their experience in the field, they scanned all the classified ads in the newspapers. Suddenly, Amir found one in particular. Several people were being asked to do telemarketing work. They went to the designated location, inside a large room where several candidates waiting patiently seated. A lady and a man appeared behind the stage.

"Good evening, ladies and gentlemen! Welcome to the world of AMWAY."

The compadres had no idea how to recruit the world, they felt as if they were locked in a movie theater earlier than a workplace. They only half understood the speaker's explanations. They wondered how they would make money without working directly for the company. The man continued his speech, showing slides to the candidates at the same time. "Do you know why big companies are present in all the countries of the world? Because they started from nothing and today, they are bathed in wealth. You wonder when that will happen to you, of course, thanks to Amway products. You can have cottages, boats, cars like that couple you see on the screen. Become a sales representative, you'll soon be a wholesaler and live in opulence."

There was absolute silence in the room, the hope of some for the work flew away like smoke. When the organizer took the floor again, he asked questions, challenging the candidates in this way:

"Could you tell me if you know of any companies that would offer you such an opportunity to make money outside of Amway?"

Convinced that he had come for nothing, a man stood up and answered:

"A toé!" (Quebecer local language) There was loud applause followed by laughter, the man took his wife's hand and slammed the door. After him, the room emptied, leaving the speaker and his companion on the platform.

A week went by and neither Martinez nor his friend had managed to find work. On Thursday evening, a numbered company called them. A company they could not remember if they had offered their service. It was another all-nighter they spent thinking about. Could this be another joke? They had no intention of falling for it again.

As soon as they arrived, the company gave them ID cards and they took note of the address they should go to. A chartered bus drove them, a few minutes later, they stopped in front of a blockade of strikers armed with placards, shouting 'no to scabs.' Martinez was stunned. Why refuse to work and go out to demonstrate when there is no work for them? Passengers got out of the bus under the jostling, a cordon of police officers allowed them to enter the building in the rain of stones, eggs and insults. Martinez received a pie in the face that blinded. This second surprise did not make him angry, the joy of working at the end was immense compared to the little pie he wiped in the bathroom.

They used the empty boxes to build mail sorting racks. The foreman made the prototype that each employee had to reproduce in several series. One day's work was enough to make the center operational. Only the mail was left.

The next day, a large delivery truck stopped in front of the building. Taken by the strikers, the driver fled under the blows of the signs and the contents of the truck were emptied into the street.

Martinez, stunned, watched this spectacle with contempt. He had never imagined that in Canada, one could destroy one's work, torpedo one's livelihood.

The second truck under police escort successfully unloaded at the dock. It was late, they were leaving the building in the absence of the strikers.

"I didn't expect such a welcoming committee for the first day of work."

"Didn't you hear what they said earlier? They're calling us job thieves!"

Martinez burst out laughing.

"Have you ever seen thieves escorted by the police to enter a building?" He retorted mockingly.

"Yes, when they plead guilty, they should be taken to jail!" Amir continued more beautifully.

"We're not at that stage. By the way, all they had to do was go home and take their seats. Is it fair that they refuse to work, while we are actively looking for working?"

"They are spoiled children, they earn big salaries and they complain, while we live on small pittances."

"We should send them to the Third World; they will come back as adults."

During the night, the sorting center was ransacked. Stickers covered the windows of the front door. The spirits warmed up in the morning, each time the workers arrived.

The insults rained down without interruption.

The calm returned; the center was opened for the distribution of mail. Several people followed one another in front of the door, equipped with identity papers to collect the franked letters. The trucks made several shuttles, the unloading team passed the mail to the preliminary sorting team, which in turn gave it to the next team until the road classification and distribution teams.

At the end of the day, the crew members were exhausted and dragged their steps toward the bus stop.

Second day of work without trouble, the atmosphere was relaxed. Martinez and his friends could take a break outside. Lunch boxes in hand, they took their place at Notre-Dame-De-Grace Park, they enjoyed their meal.

Not far away, a man their age swallowed his sandwich, Martinez ran to his rescue with a bottle of water in his hand. Leaning against his chest, the man was coughing at the top of his lungs, writhing in pain. "Take a sip of water!" Martinez begged him.

David found his breath; he had a smile on his face.

"Thank you for your help, Martinez, I almost died."

"It's a must to reach out to someone who is drowning."

It was the beginning of a friendship between the comrades and David. They met after work, they went to the movies together, they did other activities that the comrades would not have dared to do alone.

On Friday morning, they got paid for the work they had done. Martinez jumped for joy. "I got my pittance, damn!" He contemplated the check like a gold ingot, a diamond that should be quickly put in safety. Many in the room did not understand all his expressions of joy for a simple payment. This small piece of colored paper returned his honor, head high, he presented himself to the bank. Martinez endorsed the check, he no longer knew whether to deposit it or keep it as a good-luck charm, a talisman that would open other business doors for him.

At chameleon's pace, he lined up, waiting his turn to have access to the cashier. When he heard the word 'next he,' didn't know if he should part with his precious piece of paper.

The woman said, "Sir! Can I help you?" It was the cashier; she saw that he wasn't going to meet her.

"Of course!" He said.

Three weeks of work passed; the strikers had ratified the agreement on the employer's offer. The immediate cessation of work in the distribution centers was one of the conditions for returning to work. It was the end of work for Martinez, David, Amir, and the others.

The anguish seized the companions, how to find another job, they had established a routine in their lives although ephemeral, increased their self-esteem. Here, they were again plunged into darkness with no future, no tomorrow.

Chapter 3

In the evening, Martinez contemplated the sky. He counted the stars. Certainly, they were more numerous than the envelopes he had handled in the center of the sorting. Suddenly, he saw a shooting star. He made a vow, that he would have a job at short time, a permanent job without fear of being evicted. When he got up from his position, it was one o'clock in the morning. Lying on his bed, sleep was slow in coming. He thought of the recklessness he and his friends showed in frightening himself from the path among the demonstrators to enter the building. He saw through this boldness, an end to isolation, a great step that would lead them to success.

On Saturday night, Martinez could not close his eyes. All his thoughts were directed toward Karen. Since his fall on the stairs, he hadn't heard from her. Why had she helped him? He wanted to get to know her better, go out with her occasionally, take her as a friend. He worried about her mother's reaction. What would she say about seeing him again after so many weeks with no sign of life? He thought he was ungrateful to those who had helped him, he blamed himself. It was eleven o'clock in the morning, was that sunny Sunday going to change the course of things?

Martinez jumped into the cab and went shopping in an unusual way. With gifts for Karen and the family, he stood in front of the door under the watchful eye of old Catherine, perched on the balcony. She seemed to want to miss nothing of the day. Martinez worried, he thought he was getting eggs in his face. The door opened, in front of him Karen had a charming smile. "It's Martinez!" she cried to her mother. She invited him to the living room, the whole family came to surround him. Martinez apologized for the time it took him to visit them. If it was up to him, he would often come to court her.

"I apologize for the disturbance, Karen."

"The whole family is happy, don't you see?"

"Thank you, Karen."

Once the greetings were made, Martinez had a rare opportunity for a one-on-one with the one who gave him insomnia. He fell in love with the sweetness that gushed from her innocent face, draining a current of passion from which his heart was carried away. A moment of silence brought them together, they were attracted like two magnets, suddenly the passionate big-bang was heard. A long kiss chained them in place. She knew at that moment that the long-awaited happiness was there. When they let go of each other, her heart beat with joy. All her soul and spirit gave themselves over to him. The bewitching of his smile drove her crazy in a deluge of caresses that she had promised to give herself the day she would let herself go in the arms of the man of her dream.

Karen's mother interrupted this delicious moment of tenderness. At the sound of her footsteps, everyone returned to his seat. They were embarrassed, they felt as if they were being watched.

"Martinez, you will stay for supper, we won't let you leave."

"Thank you, madam, I'm going to warn my friends that I'm in the good hands. Can I use your phone?"

"Of course!" She answered.

Martinez trembled with hands, all his attention, his whole mind was somehow imprisoned in love, in the conquest of his tender heart. He left his friends a message on the answering machine. Words could not describe the touching welcome he received when he entered Karen's house.

Snacks, coffee, tea, littered the table, the whole family joined him again to enjoy the foods.

"I don't know how to thank you, madam."

"Call me, Mama Anne, welcome."

Karen let the joy show through. She asked and received permission to take a walk with her host.

They walked along Jarry Street toward the only attraction park named Jarry. What to tell her companion? She who had been discreet since her arrival in Canada confessed for the first time her feelings toward Martinez. With an uncertain step, she let herself be taken by the hand. Martinez had the impression of dragging her. How far will this sudden relationship go, unknown that she held the rudder? She had the impression that this romance, this exciting new love affair made her want to live. They stopped in the middle of a path surrounded by flowers. Martinez picked one, he planted it on her hair, their lips thought they were in a long kiss.

"Martinez," she cried out in an uncertain voice. When he answered, she lost her idea. She kept a moment of silence and then resumed. "Look me in the eyes, can you read what I'm about to tell you?"

He was embarrassed, he couldn't make things up through those piercing glances which nevertheless let his real desires be seen.

"Help me guess, I'm afraid I'm going to disappoint you."

"From the moment I saw you, a flame was lit in my heart, I knew that you were the one who would make me happy in this land."

"Did you really?"

"I am in love with you."

"I'm in love with you too. I haven't stopped thinking about you since you took care of me."

"So, we have the same thought. Loneliness is killing us; we have to unite our life to fight it."

"I'm very happy about it, this is my lucky day. I want too, but what would your mother say? We just met."

"She would be delighted; it would be the best news of her life."

Karen pushed, a long sigh, an emotion of certainty came to feed her hopes. She began to caress his hairs, his face, she stretched her lips in search of a victory kiss. The return trip was quicker than the outward journey. Karen hurried to tell her mother the news. She left Martinez with her brother; she was going to help Mom Alice set the table for dinner. She didn't know where to start in the midst of all this excitement. She was already thinking about the wedding preparations, the guests, the excitement. She was thinking about what her dress should be, what kind of suit she would choose for this unique occasion in her life. Alice read in her daughter's face that something extraordinary had happened; it had never been Karen's habit to refrain from talking about anything. This time she expected good news, she wanted to let her to tell the good news. As she thought about it, she stopped cleaning the dishes and told her:

"Mama, it's done, it's done!"

"Yes!" Alice replied, "It's drawn in your face."

"Then tell me what it is."

"You've agreed to get married, haven't you?"

"Good guess, your intuition is right. From now, you have a son-in-law! You used to tell everyone I'm an old girl, now go tell them I'm not, I have a suitor!"

"My goodness! I am not going to the streets of the United Nations and announce through the rooftops that my daughter has just found a future husband. It wouldn't make sense."

"You have no idea how much fun I will have watching the two old gossips perched like ravens on the verandah watching all my gestures and movements. They looked at their watches when I went out, they looked at them again when I came home."

" These old ladies get bored all day long, at least you make their life useful."

"Laughing at me like hyenas? No, thanks! I'll go and have a word with them!"

"Above all, no troubles in my street! Did you hear that?"

Karen dropped the plate she was holding in her hand and ran to the exit. Outside, she faced Catherine and Ellen. One of them took the initiative to speak loudly and clearly about the man they saw entering her house. The other held her back, preferring to let Karen get right to the point.

"Old girl! Speak up! Tell us what has become of him. Had he gone out the back door the good man? Ha! Ha! Ha! Ha!" Ellen screamed.

"If he went out by the back door, it's because he found you awful, he doesn't want to cover himself with shame!" Bidding Catherine.

Karen was stung alive, the worst insult she never heard since her early teens. She was thinking about how to get revenge, how she could send them on a punitive expedition. But before all that, she was shouting her displeasure.

"Wait until I catch you sneaking into the park, I won't pay dearly for your old badger skin!"

She threw everything she could get her hands on toward them. Stones, pieces of wood that a carpenter had left behind after finishing his work. She went and fetch and throw eggs to quell her anger.

Catherine received three broken eggs in her face, she hurriedly left her rocking chair, went back to her apartment, followed by Ellen. She wiped herself in vain, splashing warm water on her face. Holding a towel in the hand, Ellen died of laughing. She didn't expect a strong reaction. She and Catherine had touched the girl's sensitive points. They honestly thought the man would have run out by the back door. In the face of this escalation, Catherine wanted to call cops. She believed that she had been abused as a helpless elderly person.

"But she is crazy, this girl! You have to call your son! He's a cop."

Ellen was shaking her hands, her feet. Sweat ran down her forehead like a waterfall. She refused to grant Catherine's request. What would she tell him? Who started it? She realized that she was at fault. Now that she lives in fear of being pushed along the way by gangs of thugs, who will ensure her safety outside her home? She, who liked to take a breath of fresh air in Jarry Park, had to content herself with only looking out the window like a prisoner behind bars.

"It's going to cost us a lot! Call your son as soon as possible."

"Are you kidding me or what? If I call my son, I'll tell him we're at fault?"

"Then, you'll bear the burden of all the evil we'll suffer. These young people will not spare us, they will blindly follow their vampire queen!" (laughter)

"She is only defending her reputation, let's admit that we provoked her, she is angry, ready to do anything, even kill us!"

"To kill us for simple jokes? You're joking."

"Open your ears, listen to the news. How many people of our age are victims of aggression, often their own children! Imagine the anger of the gangs of thugs! We are dead! We are dead!"

Cathy of her little nickname, had a shiver when she heard the word kill. Faithful to herself, she believed that she had the right to create conditions for the enjoyment of her dull life. The right to provoke, to shout, and even to insult for pleasure.

"Listen, Ellen, she will never carry out her threat, she only showed us her frustration at not having a man at the foot of her bed every night! Poor little silly girl, it should be awful her dreams. If I could, I would get into her gray matter, I would flip through her thoughts page by page. I would hold her secrets in captivity, her ideas, her love projects, make her go around in circles without absolute results…Here! Yours!…We will contact the witch, the one who used to live in this building. It is said that she had transformed her old husband into a rooster that she later devoured him. He is declared dead, no one saw his body, nor attended his funeral."

"Where do you get all these sordid stories? Do you still believe in witchcraft? You will go by yourself."

"I see, you're afraid of being licked by the young people. What do you say if we pay a few of them for our protection? Let's say a few arm-wrestlers. They could break the legs of this scoundrel; it would be less dangerous in the wheelchair. As for us, we would sing the hymn to joy! Ha! Ha!"

"Where will you lock up his brothers? They alone form the most fearsome gang in the United Nations."

"I told you and I repeat It's time to get your son out of your closet! He will harass them; he will throw them in jail."

"Where do you think you are? In a dictatorial country? Old jumped-up, indecent!"

"Bin! There are plenty of alibis. He can always slip hashish, opium or any narcotic into their pocket. He could accuse them afterward. How stupid you are?"

"No, thanks!"

"In this case, you will go out alone, not with me! That means until they crucify you…Imagine at your age that they tie you to a stake, beat you, rape you, make you go through all the torments…What horror? Just thinking about it gives me goose bumps."

"Stop your manipulation! I've heard enough of you today!"

"Old pig, I can see the pleasure gushing out of your eyes when I said the word rape. Poor me! If only God had given me children, they would know how to defend me with their body and soul…I will never be at the mercy of anyone (she burst out laughing)."

"But you are completely crazy! If you want to be penetrated, put an announcement in the newspaper, men will parade in front of you, they will free you from your sexual suffering."

"I forbid you to talk to me like that, you are hiding things in your life from me."

The psychosis took hold of two gossips, Catherine took care to lock her door. With her nose stuck to the window, she had become a detective. She watched Karen's apartment, noting her every move. When she saw the little brothers in front of the door with a bag in their hand, she started to scream.

"That's it! They're sounding the death knells! Now, you have to make up your mind, call the police or die!"

Ellen went back to her apartment without saying a word. Soon after, someone rang her doorbell. Fearlessly, she asked:

"Who are you?"

"Daniel, Daniel Sahel the dean old Negro of Unite Nations. Have you forgotten that I had to come at this hour?"

"Hurry up, come in! I don't want the storyteller Cathy seeing you the whole town will know we're fucking!"

"Oh! Doesn't she have a date?"

She threw herself into his arms, she kissed him tenderly, she stopped him from talking. She would like to hear words of love; she would want to escape through her feelings. He heard her say:

"You drive me crazy, old Negro."

His sweet voice brought out the passion of seeing him naked, his chest against his own. All together, they condemned their souls to the seventh heaven, a paradise regained from where they seemed to bathe in the water of youth. It would be strong, their bodies merged in the spell of orgasm that transformed her into a chenille, then into a butterfly flying over his man. He heard her moaning in a sung voice, once she uttered the cries of joy.

"I love you, old Negro! Yes, I love you. I'm jealous, I don't want to lose you my treasure, my secret garden. Don't listen to the crazy Cathy, she will try to divide us."

"I'm jealous too, my love, I almost had a heart attack when a young tomcat was bragging about having fucked the old ladies of the area. I said no! Not my Ellen. I ran like an athlete; I was seeing you."

In spite of the delicious time they had, the old Negro noticed that Ellen was not on his plate. Worried, he took her in his arms and kissed her at length. He helped her vacuum and prepare the meal. Humor replaced the sadness he saw in her eyes. Ellen found her radiant smile again, she was not able to resist longer to the attraction of the charismatic old Negro, endowed with great admirable qualities. She stuck, she became again the teenager who, in order to show herself, impregnated herself with the masculine smell, proof of belonging to the one she was flushing her eye on. Daniel's presence reshaped her life. At no time did she think that a man of this generation could keep his sexual power intact, his openness and passion for cooking. She was thinking back to the time when she was married. Doing the dishes came back to the women, cooking came back to the women, cleaning came back to the women. She saw in her face the life she had led when she had just gotten married. She saw how difficult it was for her to get into bed with the man she hadn't chosen. Making love was a nightmare, opening her legs against her wishes was a rape she could not denounce. The pleasure that the man who shared her life took from it gave her other burdens. That of carrying children, educating them, providing for their every whim. She thought of miracles, the old Negro brought her back to the stage of sexual satisfaction. She rediscovered sex as an element of pleasure, to blossom fully was something she hadn't experienced thirty-eight years ago. She saw Daniel as an insurance, a security. He is known and respected in the neighborhood.

Day after day, Catherine returned from outside loaded with shopping bags. Halfway there, a group of young people intercepted her, took her bags and her pairs of glasses. It was a great disaster, Cathy called for help. She couldn't see without her glasses; Karen's name came out of her mouth. She was angry, she called the cops. When she got home, everything was at her door.

"Madam, nobody robbed you!" Cathy got angry; she would like to hear the cops tell her that they would put these kids to the jail.

"Go to their house! Give me back my things!" She persisted.

"Madam, your things are in front of you, don't accuse people without proof. They might pursue you for defamation."

She fumbled, one of the cops handed her glasses. She was stunned, how could these young people be courteous and tear off her glasses, leaving her blind in the street? The cops were leaving, Karen came out of her apartment, she said:

"Hey, old lady! You got a warning today, imagine what they'll do to you if you don't shut your filthy mouth!"

"The cops will come back and get you! Word of honor. You'll pay for your crime, bitch!"

"I have the impression that you didn't understand me, expect another lesson, old bastard! Next time, we'll strip you in the park, we'll take off your glasses, we'll leave you naked!"

Cathy took a dozen of eggs, she threw from her balcony in the direction of Karen.

"You want a war, you'll get it, little mangy bitch!"

Karen ran toward her, she seemed to join her on the balcony.

"I will kill you, old carcass!"

Cathy screaming at the top of her lungs.

"I forbid you to enter! I'm calling the cops!"

"Dirty coward, you're finished now!"

Cathy locked her door, jumped on the phone. She called Ellen, asked her to do the same. The pleasure she wanted to give herself by provoking Karen brought her more trouble than joy. Ellen, in Daniel's arms, answered her:

"Stop bothering me…You know what I mean?"

"I'm in danger!"

"Call the cops! I'm busy!"

"Doing what? Come out immediately, I want to see you!"

Spoiled by the old Negro; Ellen hung up her phone. She enjoyed the sensual massage nonstop of her man, leaving Cathy anger. Karen watched them through the balcony, she nodded her shoulder; her laugh caught old Negro's attention. He put his clothes back and went to meet her.

"Why had she gotten so angry? She is the wise girl of the United Nations!"

Ellen burst out laughing, she knew too much about Karen. She still feel guilt, she decided to confess, he listened to her.

"We spied her, we laughed at her, we called her an old girl without a husband. We made her an object of leisure. I confess that is the reason of her anger at the point she would like to kill us. I agreed we putted ourselves in the trouble. We found our life flat, nothing to do than staying in the balcony, laughing at the people. Especially Cathy, talking badly about others was her job at full-time. We had thrown away the rosaries to devote ourselves to mundane things that only made us feel lonely. If it weren't for you, I would be just as confused as she is right now. If you know Karen, make sure she doesn't release her gang on us." The old Negro took a long walk to find Karen on the street. He approached her and slipped her a note about Martinez.

"Hello, miss!" She turned around and was speechless. She greeted him on the head, one would have thought that she wanted to finish once and for all with these old ladies.

Politeness overcame anger, she threw down the objects she was holding in the hand. She greeted Daniel shyly. Karen was afraid that Daniel would report his state of mind to the man who would share his life. She had been having some discomfort.

"Hello, sir!"

"News travels fast, I learned that…" she answered at the same time.

"Martinez and I engaged for marriage."

"Congratulations! You are barricaded. Itinerant love is not benefits. I've known you for a long time, you're a good girl."

"Can you believe it?"

"Of course, I do! You used to help all the old ladies with the shopping as you passed them."

"You mean the hateful old lady sitting on her balcony?"

"I'm talking about all the old people. Forgive them, you have to learn to forgive. Sometimes, the spirit of revenge drives us to act in the extreme against our will. We become a prey in turn when we enter this vicious circle. Go! Go home, ignore them, they will ignore you."

"Thank you, sir!"

Leaning on his cane, the old Negro shrugged his shoulders. He did not understand the spirit of vengeance that young people had nowadays, he wondered why he wanted to attack two defenseless old women who were bored day and night, for lack of real distractions. If he could, he would take care of each of the widows in black tunics who were unwillingly parading around, going shopping or going to church.

He saw in them an extraordinary beauty for his age, a real waste, thinking that they had their skulls filled by the priest's words, that once the husband passed away, they became un-fucking women.

He turned his head; his gaze was fixed on the two gossips. He smiled and then greeted them with his hand without saying a word. He thought he was the ideal lady-killer, he believed that they were suffering from loneliness, deep down, they would want to subscribe without hesitation to a passionate escape, which could revive their sexual appetite that had been asleep for a long time, being doctrine by religion. It was Ellen's secret garden, although it was he who watered her. In front of the others, they did not know each other, they were strangers.

He took a step forward, but he couldn't go on his way without approaching the gossips. Silent, they watched him walk toward the entrance of the building. Ellen knew too much, she pretended to be innocent.

He offered them lots of activities that could occupy their day. From there, they would get to know other worlds and expand their circle of friends. Are they ready to live such an adventure? Are they willing to go out just to go to church, go shopping or go to the park to get some fresh air? Leisure activities were not their strong point. The old Negro sneezed; he took a handkerchief out of his pocket to wipe himself. He asked and obtained permission to sit down. Perched on a small stool that the gossips took pleasure in letting their feet rest on. He looked charming, winking at one or the other. He couldn't believe that they were an extinct star. He saw himself invested with an impossible mission to bring these ladies back to earth, to connect them to daily life. He improvised conversations, one of the gossips hardly ever listened to him. She whispered to Ellen:

"What a shame to see a nigger on our balcony! People will give us bad press!"

Ellen did not like insults, the word nigger referred to her clandestine lover, Daniel Sahel. Kathy was fed up with hearing the nonsense of this old man who kept wiping his pairs of glasses hanging on his neck. He took out of his pocket a newspaper with crumpled pages. He rummaged through it, he found activities for the golden age. No sooner had he said a word than she exploded.

"You, old bastard! Do you take us for old women? Go away! Get out of here you're not welcome here anymore!"

Shocked, Ellen couldn't believe her ears, how could she dare to say such nonsense to a man who wanted to do them good? She encouraged the old Negro to continue. Kathy felt embarrassed, she slammed the door and shut herself in her apartment.

"Your neighbor, is still in a bad mood?"

"Ah, don't mind her, she hates men."

The old Negro scratched his head, dandruff was falling on his shoulders. He looked away, looking for the words to justify what he was going to say without hurting Ellen. He was thinking mostly of the consequences of a clumsy statement that would end the only woman who still cared about him. Swallowing his saliva askew, he coughed for a long time, his lungs felt as if they were going out of his throat, and a glass of water was served to him. When he regained his strength, his audacity returned.

"Listen! Is your girlfriend allergic to men? Has she ever had one in her life before?"

"To tell you the truth, I really don't know her life, I met her in this building, she boasted that she was the widow of several men who would have beaten and tortured her during her youth. She had taken revenge on them now that they are out of harm's way."

"You mean she had physically liquidated them?"

"She had sold their souls to a witch she had known for years. She's dangerous, don't go in public with her."

"Don't worry, I have talismans against witches. In Africa, we are the champions of witchcraft. Especially, the villagers, those we call country people are dangerous! They can turn you into a donkey, they will use it to carry the millet or peanut harvest to the market. When I was little, I saw a peasant transforming a frog into a horse at the foot of a big Baobab! He rode on the horse and disappeared into the Baobab."

"Wow! It's scary!"

Ellen had her breaths cut off, what kind of a mess had she gotten in to? Her girlfriend would have exterminated her men, her lover is the owner of the talismans. She took out of her bag, a crucifix that she discreetly held in her hand. Would the little Jesus on the cross protect her from the talismans? She thought of its magical reach, it could be evil. However, she was living as a gossip with a witch's follower. The one who controlled the souls of her clients, destroying them for a small fee. An unofficial function that the sum received escaped to taxes collectors.

"You are safe," Daniel Sahel continued.

"So, are you a sorcerer too?"

"No, not at all! I am protected against sorcerers, I am not a sorcerer, the talismans you see are fighting against sorcerers."

"And the witches?"

"Also! They strike them down, they become dead leaves."

"Oh my! The witch of Cathy should fear you."

The old Negro went back to his native Africa, his hometown where traditional justice condemned witches. He was young when his sister was a victim of a witch. She was losing blood at the country hospital, the doctor, a cooperant did everything he could without result. He gives intravenous solutions. Her mother visited all the healers in the village, she came across one, he communicating with the spirits. The man was old as the earth, sitting on the tanned hide of a black sheep. He had his red eyes out of the sockets and motioned to Kadijatou to take place on the stool. Before she said a word, the sorcerer told her what she looking for.

"Your daughter is a prisoner of a witch."

"How did you know? I haven't told you anything yet."

"I can see from afar; you have visited many before coming here."

"Absolutely!"

"I communicate with the spirits of the elders, the exact science of witchcraft."

"I'm impressed."

"I want to save little Mariamatou, I ask for six big sheep a big bag full of millet."

"My daughter will regain her health?"

"The great sorcerers are not mistaken; their predictions are accurate. Bring what I ask you, everything will be fine!"

"I thank you in advance, master of the occult sciences, I will return with what you ask for."

- Kadijatou ran with all her legs, in one day, she fulfilled the conditions of the sorcerer. Wearing a large multicolored boubou, a African uniform. His arms stretched to the sky, holding a gourd, he pronounced words that Kadijatou did not understand. Suddenly, a smoke came out of the gourd. The smoke surrounded him and then took a direction. He followed it until it dispersed, and he took a sip of the water remaining in the gourd made of calabash, he said:

"Kadijatou, you have an evil neighbor, she feeds on your daughter's blood."

"A neighbor? How could she?"

"Look at the water in the gourd, you'd see a big, dangerous lady."

Kadijatou plunged her head into the gourd, she opened her eyes wide, she saw nothing. She scanned the walls of the bowl suddenly, she started to scream.

"The fatso Kaltoum! I saw her in the gourd!"

She returned to the village; she sounded the knells. Men, women and children beat Kaltoum, tied her up, locked her in the house and set fire. Poor Kaltoum had a terrible death, even for a witch. Miraculously, her death healed Mariamatou. It was a story that gave Ellen goosebumps. Back on earth, the old Negro was thinking of the gossip

Cathy. He thought she was a lesbian, according to him, a woman is only born for men, lives with men, has intimate relationships with men, she should not go against nature. This thought was still shared by the people of old generation. His second thought was that of treating Cathy the black widow of the United Nations. The one who kills, mates for inheritance. He had a shiver, he thought he was escaping well, he who had always watched over her. He looked in his head for the magic number, how many men had she eliminated? Ten? Fifteen? Twenty? Considering her age. Cathy came out of her apartment; she was astonished that they were talking about her. She had the impression that this old fool was in the pay of the cops, for having insisted so much on her life as a widow. She went straight to the point.

"Are you interested in my life as a widow? Do you want me to tell you how many I've killed? That's my business!"

She took her place on the rocking chair that cracked with each of her movements, she was angry. The anger bubbling inside her, Ellen asked:

"By the way, you had killed some…I would rather say how many men had you loved before they disappeared from this world?"

Cathy became very angry, she got up from her chair and pointed at Ellen. Her face reddened with anger, she looked like she'd drunk a barrel of alcohol.

"Listen, old girl! Men are like lemons; once you squeeze the juice you throw away the skin! Have you kept lemon's skins in your closet?

No!

It takes a bitch to keep the same man to warm her bed! Once they no longer satisfy me, I change them. Nothing is easier for a beautiful woman to attract a man she wants to have on her bed, by showing him a half of her bare thighs. And I can tell you that they'll take the bait for sure!"

Daniel Sahel stared at Cathy from head to toe, thinking that he had had too much, he thought, for a frail woman who brags like that. He came out of his hinges of the enraged male, he dared to raise his voice. He made her feel that she hadn't met men capable of setting her up as she merit.

"Among the dead men, in memory of whom you wear your black tunic?" He asked.

"Ah, you interested? Well, in memory of all of them, the wicked as well as the good, I reap only the annuity of the one who earned the most! Does that satisfy your curiosity, old Negro?"

"It's because you didn't get the best of man that would put you in the coffin before you committed, all that nonsense! You are a race of vipers! You deserve the gallows!"

In fact, Daniel Sahel deflated very quickly, he remembered the thousand discussions he had in the café about women's freedom, he remembered his words that he lived in a country of women, made by men for women. And that it is enough for one of them to barely scream when an armada of lawyers and enforcement officers surrounded her. He thought it best to avoid the subject and move on to things that might be good for him. The wink he gave to Cathy was to Ellen, his mistress.

Chapter 4

Daniel left his old newspaper in his hand and headed to the bus shelter. Peacefully reading his magazine, an angry couple was standing beside him. The lady was emptying her heart, she said: "They're everywhere, they have priority over everything, we satisfy their every whim, I wonder if we shouldn't leave our country and come back as immigrants. Perhaps, it would be easier for us, we too could cry out for racism and injustice!" The man at his wits' end glanced at the Dean, who was always absorbed in his reading, and his wife added: "They are sacred, untouchable. We are linguistic minorities in an ocean of English culture, no one feels sorry for us."

The couple's cry of desperation had not been heard anywhere; they lost control of their property to the United Nations. The tenants were moving the walls, opening new doors to other homes to facilitate movement between families.

The old Negro heard the conversation, he raised his head. Smiling, he said:

"Yes, I agree with you! We must build and not destroy."

The man could not believe his ears, as he watched him stand up, folding his newspaper before greeting him.

"We behaved badly toward you; we apologize."

"My grand-father said: 'Who apologizes condemns himself.' I have a little cousin who gives me moral lessons, he thinks like you. His young age didn't stop him from spitting out the big chunks to us. At each visit, he told me, we withdrew into ourselves with our cultures, our ways of life. We tend to impose it on the majority without worrying about our integration. He also said that we sound the alarm at the slightest criticism, at the slightest gesture coming from people like you. Now, I share his opinion."

Amazed, the man and his wife thought they heard someone other than the old Negro talking.

"You are the only immigrant who thinks this way, we have known many of them as tenants, whether they come from any country they act the same way."

"It's a small world," said the Dean. "You will find others, few of them will take care of your property as if it were their own. It's normal to let off your anger when you're in such situations."

They were exchanging addresses before getting on the bus. The sadness appeared in the old Negro's deep gaze, "the good of others is sacred," he murmured. He rang the stop bell, waved his hand to the couple, and left, leaning on his cane.

The couple had respect for the old Negro, never an immigrant was as open as he was. Criticizing his own was hardly the strong point of those they knew before. They saw in him a sleeping lion slowly waking up in his kingdom. On him, they thought they will be building an empire that they would use to regain the real estate they lost control over.

The outspokenness, the hangover, the viper's tongue that the old Negro had were their assets.

Two weeks later, a black Cadillac was driving slowly through the crowded streets of the United Nations. You would have thought that the Queen of Canada came to visit all the nations in their homes. When it came to stop, others thought they saw movie stars or popular singers coming out. But in fact, what would a wealthy person looking for in that miserable corner? When the driver's door opened, people were massed at the entrance of the building, on the balconies could not believe their eyes. Elegant, the man rushed into the building, brought out the old Negro leaning on his cane, wearing a traditional African outfit. He displayed a rare cheerfulness which gave the word of head to his neighbors. How could he have climbed a rung, a situation as colossal as having a luxury car, a private driver? What this old man hiding? Who does he work for? Could him be some kind of undercover agent to better unmask his own? A traitor or an honorable man? Questions rained down on some, while others showed him unconditional respect.

Daniel Sahel of his own name was astonished by all this honor reserved for statesmen, how is it possible to own such a beautiful car and not use it to take public transportation that he thought was reserved only for puppets of his kind?

"Riding in this luxury thing, life is beautiful. When you stop, I will film myself with this car for my friends in Africa!"

"This is America, you can get one."

"Bah! In another life maybe, I missed everything in this one. By the way, where are you driving me? Are we still in the Montreal Island? I feel like we're somewhere else! Where is this corner?"

The man had a smile that reminded his wife that their guest did not venture outside the United Nations. She wanted to be clear-headed, she asked him:

"Is this your first trip away from home?"

Daniel Sahel was scratching his chin, he seemed distraught in everything around him, he was dreaming of the day when his life would change, the day when destiny would stop before him to approach him, to tell him that his turn had come, that he deserved to live in opulence. He would console himself with this dream, when he looked at his age; he felt sorry for himself. If he could, he would go back in time, he would stop him at the age of his youth in order to get back on the right path of life, to acquire all those possessions that obsessed him. He came back to himself; he answered the woman.

"Excuse my curiosity, madam, I am like a child taking the train for the first time. I love everything that passes in front of me, there is no such thing at the United Nations."

"You call the United Nations the Park-Ds extensions?"

"Well…The United Nations here it is ha-ha! A corner dedicated exclusively to a diversity of different nationalities, in fact almost all the earth finds refuge there."

"And you, you are its ambassador plenipotentiary?"

"I am Daniel Sahel, the oldest of the neighborhood known as the Old Negro."

"The revered master among his people! We are happy to hear a person like you, appreciate his host country. You are a unique case; you will help us understand all this beautiful world. We were used to hearing rather the voice of those who shout racism, never compliments as you do.”

When they asked him what he did before he retired, his body was cold, one would think he was at the North Pole. They just touched what had haunted him relentlessly for years. Work, a scary name, a name that gives him goose bumps.

“In my native country, I was a high-ranking civil servant. Here, I can’t find a job to match my knowledge. Little by little, laziness settled in, it invaded my body, mind, she governed me, she decided everything I should do, leaving me no choice. Could I say that at sixty-five years old we are finished? Nothing to do and that all the doors are closed to me?”

The woman Thought differently.

“It’s not too late to find a job adapted to your age, your ability. You are healthy, I will give you forty-eight years.”

Daniel Sahel took what he heard as a joke. Flattery is an art that seduces momentarily, he was not certain that it would turn into a real fact under the circumstances.

“Do you have one for me, madam?”

Happy to have led him directly to the goal, the woman turned from her seat and winked at him. His old heart almost stopped, he was burning with impatience to know if this joke as he had originally believed it would turn into a job? A job for a man leaning on the cane. He was testing his hosts, he asking the question whose answer could not be indirect.

“Do you have one for me?”

The man also glanced at him, displaying a broad smile. He suddenly appeared worried about how the old Negro would react if he had to give him the job description. He ended the suspense after much thought.

"Of course! This is up to you, sir!"

The old Negro was gloating, he didn't expect an offer that fell from the sky.

"Me? Me, Daniel Sahel? The old Negro of United Nations?"

"Yes, you, sir!"

"Wait a little while, stop rolling."

"But you look sad to us."

"No! Not at all! You just healed me with a magic wand! Now, my heart is overflowing with happiness. Sir! Madam! I think you're wonderful. I have just triumphed over idleness!"

The car stopped beside de street, he stuck his head out then cry of joy. They arrived at the house, and what property? What an immense yard? Everything seemed unreal, enchanted as in a fairy story. Is this the house of the President of the Republic? At table for dinner, the man gave him the details of the long-awaited work.

"We appoint you concierge of our building located at the United Nations in your undisputed kingdom."

"At the United Nations? A building located at the United Nations?"

"Yes, sir. What do you think of it?"

"I accept it with joy!"

He got up from the chair, went to shake the man's hand, gave hugs to the woman.

"What is the job?" He asked.

"Collect rents, make small repairs."

"What a wonderful job!" The best career of old man like me! Wow! That's really a great news.

"We pay you seven hundred dollars a month."

"Really?"

"And free housing!"

"Wait a minute, you are giving me heart attack! What a service!" Daniel Sahel can't believe his ears, what would say his world in the United Nation? They wouldn't believe.

When he met them, he singing one of his songs reserved for happy days, he gave up his cane, did a few dance steps then said:

"Listen to me! Listen brave men! You who challenge winter, spring, summer and fall to make men of you! Valiant men who make themselves useful, who are useful for society! I announce you that…I have just landed what is called a job! Yes, from now, I am the janitor of a building at the United Nations! Finally, a job, what a pleasure!"

The companions were speechless. How did it cost to succeed in this hat trick? No one gave him the courage to even commit himself to the job of newspaper delivery, so he made the bad mouths lie. Sitting on his rocking chair, he sometimes took his pipe, sometimes his coffee, savoring this little happiness so much dreamed of that had been slipping through his hand for years. Suddenly, the doorbell rang, he got up, opened to an old friend.

"Oh, what a dress code! A diplomatic valise…enter his excellence, welcome to you!"

"Thank you, Daniel, we haven't been seen for several months, how are you old Negro."

"Better than yesterday! And the day before yesterday! Can I offer you a coffee?"

Gabriel got carried away:

"You don't offer yourself brandy anymore? Stop dilating your coffee cup!"

"As you can see, I'm broke."

"You will never change, sacred Negro!"

"So, what do I owe this visit?"

"I'm was passing through, I thought I'd pay a visit to my old friend, here you are, you can't even offer me a drink."

"Forget the drink, just have my coffee. Tell yourself, Gabi, that I'm not the old Negro you used to know! I'm reorganizing my life."

"Oh! May the Africans dead listen and support you, reorganizing your life when you have one foot in the grave is a miracle from God! You want to become young again, do you intend to get married? Ha! Ha! Ha! Listen, old Negro! I have three children, a woman in my life!"

Daniel Sahel raised his head in the air, giving the impression that he was looking for his words. His old eyes saw far away, he came back to haunt Gabriel with his questions.

"With this uniform, this valise, I suppose you hold an important position in life."

"I'm looking for work, old bastard!"

"You don't work, how can you feed three children and a wife Gabi?"

"They are to the care of the state, old Negro!"

"It is immoral."

"Immoral you said? If the society in which we live give me a job, I don't ask them to feed me, nor my family. They putted my job request and my diploma in the garbage because I am a dirty immigrant, I don't have Canadian diploma or experiences."

"It's cruel to give birth to children to increase the social benefit."

Daniel Sahel had set fire to the powder with this last sentence. Gabriel dropped his suitcase on the floor, standing up he cried, he seems like he was going to beat the old Negro, a great talker. He unloaded everything he had in his heart.

"What cruelty are you talking about, old Negro? My father did not educate me, he is illiterate. From my early childhood, I knew nothing but misery, I walked twenty kilometers on foot to go to school in another village. Poorly dressed, I had neither lunch nor a school bag. Often the rain came down on me, wetting all my school supplies. I was falling in the mud. I was laughed at, the teacher sent me away because I was dirty. But here, in this beautiful country, they don't need me with all that they have at their disposal. Schools in the neighborhood, school buses, psychologists, teaching aids, they even offer them food, where is your problem, old Negro?"

"But you're not in Africa, my little boy! Everyone sees to the education of their children."

"You talk too much, you talk badly. I'll take you to my house, instead of chatting you could educate them."

"Drive me? You didn't come by bus?"

"My car is just parked in front of your door, follow me to the balcony."

"Did you stole it?"

"Shut up, ugly face once and for all!"

Gabriel took it by the shirt collar, he dragged him to the balcony.

"Look at all these cars, point out the one that goes with my character."

Released, Daniel Sahel pointed to an old car that had been in an accident, the rusty doors having multiple paint colors.

"I can't think of another one that would go better with your character, little madman!"

"My outfit looks like this car? Choose another one! A little respect, please."

"You want to tell me that this car in the middle is yours!"

"Ha! Ha! Ha! This is America, man! It drives with the best marks."

"How did you get it? Do you sell the drugs? Which bank would lend money to a parasite like you?"

"It's a secret!"

"Are you armed robbery?"

"Shut up, old fool!"

"Bah! Take it from the Dean, I'm the only one biting the dust in everything, even the lazy ones have their cars…huh? Life is the most unjust thing in our world. Should we take it as a comrade? So that it spares me from suffering? Should I smile at her so that she can push luck into my arms?"

Daniel Sahel continued to raise his head when he saw Gabriel take Cuban cigars out of his briefcase. He gave him one and then lit his own. The phone ringing, it was Annie. She invited the Dean to eat his exotic dish. He let himself be led by Gabriel, dragging his extinguished cigar to his lips.

"My sister! This is Gabriel."

"Enchanted, Gabriel!"

Gabriel knelt down, lovingly kissing Annie's hand. He wished to see her somewhere alone in his company. What would it take to see this dream come true? A woman of this beauty could escape him very quickly, it was necessary to be careful not to reveal his love for her.

"Beautiful woman, call me Gabi, it's humbler and sensual."

Annie had a flash, she stared at him, she tried to put him in a contest. Quickly, the memory came back to her.

"Oh! I know you, you used to juggle with women in the street."

"That's indisputable! I am the only male capable of satisfying all the women of your generation."

"My little sister, I think you're confusing him, he looks more like a businessman than a juggler. Come on! I want to show you his car."

Annie went back to the kitchen with her head down, she was amazed that a simple juggler could run over gold while she was working to lose her breath, yet the fruits of her labor do not turn to gold.

"We would have seen it all! A juggler metamorphoses into a businessman can only live on scam. In other words, everything falls to him from the sky, he bends and picks it up."

Gabi smiled, he annoyed Annie, his wink threw the powders to the fire. He remembered her; he called her the beautiful North Star. Elegant, wearing high heels, leaving no man indifferent. From her rhythmic walk, her bewitching silhouette gave the impression of detaching her body with each step. The eyes tirelessly fixed on her, he tried to possess her soul, touching her round ass like a balloon, her breasts real pointed cones, doddering, real fetishes made him crazy.

"Crazy, Negro! Allow me to deliver your sister from her loneliness, a beautiful woman should not be without a husband for a long time, fearing that she will wither like an unwatered flower. I dream of gluing her, of putting my tongue on her lips…"

"My sister? Going out with a vagabond? That never then."

"Old, weak Negro, I imagine your cassava is cooked, you no longer swim in the immense ocean of pleasure that women carry. We are in the country of free women, get out of my view old man, I'm going to talk to her! (He pointed at her)."

"Look at me, doll! Am I not beautiful enough to torment you? What are you going to do with this appetizing body? A man has to make it his own in order to satisfy his sexual need! Allow me to swim inside your ocean and dive left, dive right, go into its depth, provoking a bewitching cataclysms of orgasms that will submerge your life forever."

"Hearing you speak, Joker, you possess the virtue of resurrecting emotionally moribund women? Do you pretend to open the door of love that I locked in hell for?"

She kept her temper, she seemed to agreement with this nonsense. The wink she made was considered as a consent, it became bold. He got up from his chair, he went to join her in her chores.

"I knew it, pretty doll, I always knew that you were waiting only for that! Yes! Here I am! Come and cuddle in my arms, I want to free you from your suffering, come take your first batch of kisses, my darling."

"Okay, Gabi. But I' m embarrassed in front of my son and my brother," she answered. "I'll make an effort if you close your eyes."

"With pleasure, beauty queen of seduction!"

Gabi closed his eyes, keeping his lips open in search of the kisses. He imagined her in a hot sensual moment and rubbed against him, like piranhas of emotion devouring him, he couldn't take it anymore, he lost his patience. She reassured him with a magical voice.

"Don't move, I'll wipe my hands, I'll give you a long kiss and roll around you!"

"I knew it, I'll be the first to taste you! I love this moment, you can't imagine, oh Annie! I feel myself in hurricane of passions."

The bottom of her panties was already wet, he was coming before she touched him. She took a glass filled with dishwater, she poured it over him, she slapped him. Gabi opened his eyes; he ran to the toilet to clean himself. The old Negro cried: "My grandfather said that when the hen pecks the chicken, they know that they have reached the limits."

Annie continued:

"Now you know how to hold your tongue?"

"You have violated my right to be a male! You humiliated me in front of your kid, your brother! If it was in my country, I would kill you right now to avenge my honor I would kill you right now to avenge my honor!"

"You would indeed? In that case, you must return to your country, here, women are stronger than you, poor fool!"

"Shut your mouth!"

"No! You must listen to me once and for all! I can accuse you of many things. Sexual touching, rape, violence and more. You'll rot for a long time in the shadow of the bars if you don't learn to hold your tongue."

Disgusted, he shook his head. His eyes were poached and he could hardly contain his anger. He resented the system that edited the conditions of women, they were untouchable, the children became kings. He became frustrated when he remembered the social worker who had come with great fanfare to check his fridge on her son's claim that there was no food left in the house. His resentment was heightened when the woman threatened to take his children away. He said, these women must have had husbands who were soft, weak-minded to the point that they put themselves above them and overwhelmed to the other men. He realized once again that he had lost, he deflated like a balloon.

Gabi wanted to drown his sorrows, so, he took a bottle of alcohol out of his second bag and put it on the table, under the astonishing gaze of Abraham. He helped himself, took a sip, and burst out laughing. He was the first to consume alcohol in this house, the first to defy the order established between Abraham and his mother.

"Why did you invite him, Uncle?" Abraham grumbled. Gabi threw the oil on the fire when he openly provoked the boy.

"Haven't you been raised to respect the adults? Little pest!"

"Yes! I don't respect drunkards."

In his mentality, facing an adult, standing up to him was a punishable outrage he could not allow. He regretted the time when women and children were subjected, beaten and silenced. He looked back on his own time; his time gone by. His face down, an anger made his hair stand up. He looked at him, shooting him with his eyes, pointing his index finger at him.

"I'll make you swallow your tongue! My children are smarter than you! They will rise above this society. But you, you will go nowhere. Unfortunately, you are not my son, if you were, I would teach you one of those lessons that you will never forget for the rest of your life."

"Will you shut up now please?" Annie cried.

"Oh, may her majesty forgive me, may she not put herself in a trance, may she allow me to edit my thoughts, however reprehensible they may be."

Daniel Sahel, the old Negro scratched his head as usual. He had heard enough of his friend's bullshit. He was looking for a way to end this discussion. The answer came from Abraham, he grabbed the bottle of alcohol and ran to empty the contents into the bowl. Gabriel entered a crisis; he shook the house.

"Give me back the bottle, now! There, your little piggy, is out of bounds!"

Laughing with joy, Abraham gave him the bottle. He sniffed and then realized that it was empty, his anger increased, he had just been deprived of his drink that he sacrificed to get it. He thought about his cash locked in the bottle, the drink would find its way back to the sewers. He imagined the rats partying, getting drunk, biting each other in disorder a few meters under his feet.

"You got your bottle, so sit down!" Said the old Negro.

"But…it's empty! You want to roll me now?"

"You're making a fuss over a bottle of liquor?"

"People kill for drugs, what's the difference?"

Daniel Sahel coaxed his friend, invited him for a drink after dinner. Once in the car, Gabi changed his mind. He had to go back to Quebec City to help his neighbor move. He dropped off Daniel Sahel, hurrying across town in a hurry.

Chapter 5

On Sunday morning, the owner of the building introduced the old Negro to the tenants of his large building. Some wished him good luck, others stared at him, they didn't say a word to him. They were already thinking of the day that they would all together kick him out of the building, and inflict the same fate on him as the previous janitor. In fact, he had to talk to them, to find solutions for good neighborhood. Many of them were not aware of his presence, they discovered it at every event.

Once installed, Daniel Sahel tackled the daily problems. Putting the building in order. Above him, a group of young people were dancing to rap music. From outside, the sound could be heard. Daniel knocked on the door without being heard, he took his master key, opened it suddenly, and went to stop the music. He angered the dreaded young people.

"Who are you?" Asked the landlord's son, surrounded by his friends, wearing backward caps. Daniel Sahel smiled a smile that said a lot about his mission, he was unwavering.

"I'm the new sheriff of the building, no more banditry! Those of you who do not live here must get out immediately!"

They went out, one behind the other, making rude gestures. Daniel Sahel put his hands in his pockets and watched them disappear from the building. He turned toward the boy, he warned him. The boy's response was overwhelming, he threatened the Dean.

"You chased away my friends! Don't forget that I am the Caïd of the gang! We'll give you a hard time! We'll set fire to your house. You need a buddy guard everywhere you go!"

Daniel remained firm, he went by his authority with these young people. The Caïd stared at him, he looked at his face matured by time, shaped by wisdom. He refused to deprive himself of his music, for him, it was a way of expressing himself freely.

"Oh! If I understand, you are all crazy people, lost in the building, emitting noise pollution. Should I congratulate your actions? Should I close my eyes and let you destroy everything? I say no! And no!"

"You have no power over us! You're wasting your time!"

Keychain hanging from his belt, Daniel Sahel seemed to have complete control of the building. He opened the door to the previous janitor who came to collect his personal belongings. The man had not accepted to be evicted, leaving room for an old nigger have been the worst judgment of his former boss. He emptied his heart:

"You have soiled my armchairs! Take off your shoes on my table! I don't see how you're more useful than me…You wouldn't last, I tell you. The same thing will happen to you in a short time! You would regret having set foot in this jungle."

Daniel Sahel listened attentively to this man on the border of depression. Could it be the behavior of the tenants that reduced him to this level? He offered him a beer and tried to calm him down.

"In fact, how much time had you spent in this jungle?"

"You have entered in a mysterious world, beware of those around you, they are real vampires, voodoo, black magic! You see I have goosebumps, they told me, yes, they warned me many times that my days are counting in this building. One week later, you replace me, what a coincidence?"

"And you believe all this bullshit?"

He approached Daniel, he blew in his ear, he afraid of the spirits reporting to them every word he said. He had the impression that his detractors spied him.

"I saw magic rituals in apartment number five. They sacrificed a white chicken, I saw the blood of this poor fowl! You know what?"

"No!"

"They were all dressed in black! Candle in hand they were going around in circle, they called out to Lucifer!"

"They did?"

"The white chicken represents me, I'm white, you see? They carried out their threats, look where I am now!"

"You tolerated sacrifices, but damn it, you should call the police!"

"Huh! The police? They seem to have them under a spell! It's rare that they stop in front of this building. Another thing, you'll never manage to collect the rents, you can't show the building, they'll stop you by all means."

"Can you believe it?"

"Of course! They even threatened to turn me into a rat! You'd better get a priest to come and remove bad spirits in this building."

"You're telling a bedtime story."

When his predecessor left, Daniel Sahel took a deep breath and lit his pipe. Born in Africa, he knew that witchcraft exists. He refused to let himself be destabilized by any rituals; he closed his eyes to all the consequences of bad spells. He crucified him on the neck and went to knock on the door of apartment number five. A half-asleep woman opened it, she yawned in front of him, she invited him to sit down in the living room. On a small table in the middle of the room between the armchairs placed opposite each other, he saw a book that gave him chills. He was trembling despite his boldness, his determination. He was beginning to believe in his predecessor's yeses. The book laid out on the small table surrounded by unlit candles, he could read on the cover page, *Grimoires and rituals of high magi*, while the woman was talking to him, he was absorbed by this book. Little by little, his fear dissipated, when he reached out his hand to take it, the woman shouted a cry that paralyzed him.

"Take your filthy hands off this book!"

Daniel looked at her with his eyes wide open, he withdrew his hand, holding his breath. His memory was blurred, he didn't know where to begin. The lady went to squeeze his precious book in the drawer, she came back to face him. He finally told her what had been burning him since the departure of the man who claimed to be a victim of witchcraft.

"I'm a bit curious!"

The lady looked surprised, what was he going to say? She was looking for his words, she was attracted by the size of the crucifix he hung on his neck. She asked him:

"If I understand, you are the priest of the building."

"Why do you say that?"

"What you put on your neck means everything."

"Oh! I'm a believer, I'm sure you are."

"What do you want? If you have nothing to say to me, get out!"

"Okay, madam! I would like to warn you that it is strictly forbidden to parade candles lite around the apartment."

He went out with his head up, headed to the entrance where the children were bickering over a baseball. Daniel grabbed the bat that one of the children was using to hit the ball, the child was holding it, did not want to give it to him. He dropped his cane, he tickled him, the boy couldn't resist, he gave up the bat.

"Go, play in the park! Here, you risk breaking the windows."

"Then give us back the stick," said the boy.

He put the stick back on and went back to his house.

It was the first of the month, that day, the Canada Post mailman with his burden entered the building. Several tenants were jostling each other on the stairs, leading up to the main entrance. As soon as the bag was dropped, it was taken by storm. Everyone left with their social benefit cheques. Daniel Sahel thought he saw a herd of elephants, crossing the road in his Africa savannah. With his hands resting against his cheeks, he sat down in front of what was left of the couriers. When he came to, he put the mail back in the boxes. There was a small parcel left, he looked for the addressee, his surprise was great. It was well intended for him. Who would send him this gift? Would it be the boss of the building? To what honor? He opened it; a smell of human excrement suffocated him. Daniel went outside to get some fresh air, thinking about the previous concierge.

Could it be the work of vampires or voodoo? He found no satisfactory answer. In front of his door, a note invited him to leave before midnight. Shortly afterward, a girl came to warn him that a door to the vacant dwelling was open. He rushed there, when he came back, he froze when he saw his chairs, his table overturned, his television thrown on the floor with the wires torn out, his documents torn, scattered on the floor, urine on the bedroom carpet, graffiti on the walls warning him that the worst was yet to come.

Dark eyebrows, he picked up his belongings on the floor "The Kid! This is the work of the Caïd, he told me so!" He grunted. The piece was big to swallow, he went out to call the woman of his life.

"Ellen! Come and see what happened to me!"

Her voice was shaking, she was afraid he might have an accident.

"Tell me before I come."

"Vandalism, my love, this building will drive me crazy!"

"Wait until I come, don't touch anything."

The cab was landing in front of the door, she noticed a grotesque insult in the hallway. She stopped to take note. Convinced that it was serious, she took a camera out of her satchel and filmed the words from all angles. The tenants thought she was a policewoman looking for evidence of wrongdoing. She went to knock on her man's door.

News of her arrival spread quickly throughout the building. Convinced that this time something serious will happen that could incriminate his son, the father of the indomitable Caïd Rhody pulled his son by the hairs. They took the corridor leading to Daniel's apartment. He stopped in front of the door, he glued his ear, he listened to what was being said inside. Suddenly, he made himself heard, he shouted:

"Open up! I bring you the culprit!"

Was this a joke? Daniel Sahel opened the door. The man almost fell on his head when he saw the extent of the damage. Rhody slapped his son twice and ordered him to clean up the mess. Ellen took the Caid out of his father's hand, she had gotten in between them.

"Don't worry, sir! I'll get him to clean up his mess! Go in peace."

"Do you think he'll have any criminal record?"

"In principle, yes! If Daniel files a complaint. Knowing him, he loves children, he wouldn't." She turned to look at him, Daniel nodded. The man went out, relieved, and went to get the beer he had left behind to take his child to the sheriff.

Above him, lived a lady with three children from different fathers. She has a bar at home and serving alcohol to men without a license, a sort of bar that the men of her ethnic group frequented. The customers went in and out as if they were at the mill. Daniel Sahel looked down on all these people. The craziest one came out singing, lowered his pants and urinated through the stairs. Others, beer bottles in hand, were bickering in front of the door. They were arguing about which one of them would spend the night with Victoria. One of them took a coin out of his pocket and each of them chose one side or the other. He tossed the coin, and when it fell, he shouted victory. Inside, cigarette smoke floated above the customers, a veritable toxic cloud poisoning the three children inside every night.

Three refrigerators lined up side by side filled with alcohol, an entire freezer adjusted, served as a reserve of drinks on weekends. With the help of his girlfriends, they served the customers. Victoria never took her eyes off the cash register. Sometimes, she hugged one person, sometimes, she hugged the other. The men engaged in sexual touching. She was slapped on the buttocks, she let her hands feel her thighs, her pubis. The skirt which she carried hardly hid her genital part. With the occasion, she denuded herself, she danced at the rhythm of the music. Running from left to right, throwing herself into the arms of her customers. This was her trademark. Attract, please, sell her merchandise.

The old Negro had troubles in his arms, the building was almost empty on weekends, those who remained didn't know where to go. He thought about the possible reproaches that would be made against him, whereas he had not hesitated for a second to put an end to the gathering of young rappers on his second day of work. One of the drinkers wandering the corridor was talking to him. He astonished to see him parading around at late hours without any precise goal, the man was talking to himself, Daniel was approaching him. With each sip of beer, it took him a few minutes before he said a word. He repeated himself, he dropped himself on the floor. Daniel Sahel was in all his moods; would he help him get up? He tried the impossible.

"Get up! Lazy, I forbid you to dirty my floor!"

The man knocked out by the alcohol began to vomit, he rolled on the floor, he grabbed his belly. He had the impression that his stomach would burst.

"Water! I want water!"

The old Negro shrugged his shoulders.

"What water? The one that turned you into an animal?"

The man stopped talking, Daniel Sahel panicked. He ran to call the ambulance. The second customer came out of the dwelling, he combined the large cigar that his lips held and the bottle of pure alcohol that he alternated. He approached Daniel Sahel as soon as he had finished cleaning the vomit from the previous night client in the middle of the night.

"Tonight, I promised myself that I would drink a big one! You know what I mean?"

"Yes! You'll finish your pacifier in the emergency room."

He approached toward the stairs; the railing was supporting him. He advanced step by step, arrived in the middle he fell down to find himself at the bottom. The broken bottle, the alcohol was spilling out everywhere, giving an additional chore. Daniel Sahel was screaming in anger; he was on his way to talk to the social bistro owner.

"Madam, I declare a curfew. Your clients must leave the premises before there is a death in the building."

Mrs Victoria turned her eyes around and stared at him. Her hands were on her hips and she said:

"What, a curfew? There is no fire in my apartment. What is an old man of your age doing at this hour?"

"I'm cleaning up your mess!"

"Did the landlord send you? Fuck you, old nigger!"

She spat in his face; she closed the door violently. Daniel froze, he didn't expect such a welcome.

That night, a battle broke out between two drunken men, causing damage to the property. Daniel Sahel had a difficult task. When the repairs were completed, he presented a large bill to the landlord. She opened the envelope and began to cry.

"Are you crazy, old nigger! Why giving me this bill!"

"You are doing forbidden trade! You have damaged the property. I hold you responsible for the damage, that's normal, madam."

"I've never paid a bill after a fight, leave me alone, it's not the last one!"

She tore up the bill and threw it in his face.

"I will chase you out of this house, you disturb your neighbors every night."

"You would go before me, I've seen the strongest ones in your place, they're all gone. Where did you come from? Did the landlord send you? Go to hell!"

A week went by without any noise in the building, the night brought its share of worries. A stranger phoned the old Negro, the man threatened him at the end of the line.

"Hello! Who's speaking?"

"Daniel! Daniel the janitor."

"Ah! The old Negro, the new sheriff himself."

"You guessed right."

"OK! I give you a piece of friendly advice. If you value your life, let Mrs Victoria alone. At the moment I'm talking to you, you owe her the sum of one thousand five hundred dollars and twenty-five cents. That's the money she's lost since the clients haven't been coming in regularly."

"Sir, Madam owed the building two thousand dollars for repairs caused by the several fights."

"This is part of the charm of this small social club, you cannot forbid it. There is a price to pay and you are the first to be sacrificed."

"Who are you?"

"Who I am doesn't matter, the most important thing is to eliminate you, to put you out of harm's way."

"So, I am waiting for you, if you are a man, I invite you to a duel in front of witnesses."

"All I want is to kill you, to deprive you of your life away from any testimony."

The threat did not materialize, the man who had made the threat disappeared into the mist, leaving Mrs Victoria in her fate. Daniel Sahel was right to swell his chest, the recourse he filed with the rent control board allowed him to kick out the owner of the speakeasy. Mrs Victoria, the fearsome one, who was quoting one by one the neighbors complaining in the laundry room. How many of them had their beaks nailed shut or risked receiving a punitive expedition? The day of her departure turned into a day of celebration in the building. Those most annoyed by the noise organized a BQ party in the backyard. The big hero was the old Negro. They congratulated him and brought him a drink. One of Mrs Victoria's four direct neighbors stopped the music and made a short speech.

"I raise my glass to the tallest man in the building, if we had him three months ago, we wouldn't have had any psychological trauma. I congratulate him for getting rid of the great plague in the neighborhood. I invite you to acquire the best mattresses for the future days, because…we will sleep well."

They raised the toast to the health of the old Negro. Is it enough for him to say mission accomplished? Daniel thought of the rest of the tenants, those who were absent from this mini party. Are they his supporters? They had never complained about the noise or the comings and goings. The relationship with them could not help but deteriorate. As a good soccer fan, he was satisfied with this one-to-zero victory. One for him, zero for the troublemakers.

Daniel Sahel gained the respect of those he freed from nightmares, there was still much to do. Relationships became strained with others who refused the established order in the building. The tone in the corridors rose with each meeting. In the evening, a terrible noise shook the building. It sounded like an earthquake. This unusual tremor caused several tenants to leave the building in a hurry. One of them described the noise just above him as an explosion. There was dust coming from apartment number ten. The old Negro rushed out; he was about to knock on the door. As usual, there is a deadly silence. He opened the door; the lights were turned off. He shouted, he wanted to make sure no one was in danger. Suddenly, he faced two men armed with construction tools.

"What are you looking for here, old nigger?" One of the men said, taking off his white helmet covered with dust.

"That's me! The old nigger asking the question!"

"Oh! Has your janitor's title gone to your head?"

"What right do you have to change this dwelling? There are rules to be respected in this building."

The two men burst out laughing, they continued the demolition during Daniel Sahel's sermons. Suddenly, the tenant dropped the hammer; he walked toward the old Negro; the drool came out of his mouth.

"Listen, old man! I shit the rules, our life is conditioned by it! The city had them, the governments had them, and now you, the Negro wants to impose yours to us? What kind of world do we live in?"

He kept his mouth shut while he searched for his words, arguments that could bring the tenant back to his senses. He also showed them that he was the one primarily responsible for this building, everything had to be seen and approved by him.

"My friend!"

"Ha! Ha! (Turning to his friend)You hear that? We are now his friend, wow! Well, I am not your friend old Negro!"

"Then, I call you, my brother."

"Are you kidding me? Listen, donkey nigger! Brothers are living in the cathedral, get out from here!"

"Stop destroying the house!"

"If you want me to send you to the cemetery, I'll do it with pleasure. Look at that saw, we'll close the door, then we'll cut you to pieces, what an atrocious death?"

The second wiped the sweat from the sleeve of his shirt, looked like a hitman. He coughed many times before returning fire.

"For ten years that he has been paying for this accommodation, it gives him the power to transform it to his taste! Go tell this to your master!"

Daniel Sahel left the house, a few moments later the police arrived, the work was stopped, the tenant accused of mischief, vandalism, he had to evacuate the house. He enjoyed his second victory in peace and quiet. Two-to-zero; his escort was soaring. He didn't expect that there would be the diehards, the tough of the tough, those who held mysterious powers. The third challenge came next day when he surprised a boy scribbling on the stairwell walls. With his head down, he could not see him coming leaning on his cane. He approached him shouting.

"Let go of that felt pen, delinquent boy!"

The boy jerked; he was not expecting a visit of this nature. He looked up, staring at the new sheriff.

"Who are you, sir? Get lost!"

"Ah! By the grace of God, I have my vandal!"

"You're not holding anything; I'm going to spray paint in your eyes!"

"Oh! Is this how you address the one who will make you a respectful man? I've already seen you with the Caïd."

"Ha! Ha! We sent you a package of shit that's not enough for you, you want another child saver?"

Daniel pulled him by the ears, he took him to his lodging. He was giving him a moral lesson.

"Open your ears, listen to me! If you need the paper to scribble, ask your parents for them. These walls are painted, we buy the paint, can you pay for it?"

The boy tried to escape, in vain, frustrated, he answered.

"You're the janitor, it's your job to clean up the mess, not me! Have you looked at the walls all over town full of graffiti? It's not the writers who clean them."

"What's your name?"

"Eric."

"How much do these markers cost?"

"A dollar and a half each."

"Do you work?"

"No!"

"How did you get it?"

"My parents work."

"What will they think of you if I charge them for the damage? I'm sure they won't be happy; imagine all the pain you would cause them?"

Eric understood the seriousness of his act, he washed the walls, removed all the graffiti. Rewarded by Daniel Sahel, he became his most rigorous right-hand man. The five dollars a week he received made him the most responsible of the boys living in the building. In the backyard, he distributed chocolate bars to his friends after the games.

"I think the sheriff of the building is nice, he's the one who gives me chocolate."

The kid of the gang shot him with his eyes, when he opened his mouth, it was to reprimand him.

"You allied yourself with this old bastard? He chased you out of my house!"

"I know, but don't you think we're exaggerating a bit? We had broken the eardrums of the whole building without respite."

The Caïd's anger was growing stronger.

"You want to help that old gimp? Get out of here!"

"Before I walk away, let's take a vote!"

"All right, all those who are not against him raise their hands!"

The surprise was great, five of six kids raised their hands. Head down, the Caid left without turning around. But by the way, the winner was the sheriff, he knew how to get the youngsters back without any effort to put them at his service.

In the night, a scream woke him from his restless sleep. A woman and her children screamed for help. He got up, put on his clothes, walked down the step. He knocked on the door. The man was not welcoming; as soon as he opened the door, he urged him to leave.

"What do you want, old rat, this is my home, I do what I like!"

"You have never reached out your hand to a person in danger?" The man pressed him against the wall.

"Don't interfere in my family affairs, do you understand? Old Negro, dirty pickle. Are you playing Gestapo in this building? But we're going to kill you! Yes, kill you without pity!"

Daniel Sahel got dizzy, he sat on the stairs hand on head, listening to the father becoming more and more dangerous. When he returned home, he called the police. Mr Valère could not believe his eyes when the police came in and handcuffed him. Outside, he escaped, was caught, thrown on the ground and lifted up in front of the neighbors. The night was short, and Valère was released in the morning with a promise to testify before the judge for domestic violence. His wife and children found refuge in an institution for battered women. There, she feared the worst. When he found his empty home, Valère went to knock at every door of the building without finding his family. He returned in his footsteps, crossed the backyard and walked around an old mattress that had been abandoned for several months. He walked in the alley, he felt betrayed, abandoned. Exhaustion and fear of tomorrow got the better of him. Here, he was leaning against a tree trunk, fists around his neck, his head between his knees, he cried out in distress. He saw the judicial system of his adopted country passing before him like a fortress of evil. This same system, he said, condemned his friend, for having used his customary law to straighten up his children who had been dragged into the streets by the gangs. Today, dispersed in different homes, they were worse than when they lived under parental authority. Without education, without a future, they became little thugs, drug dealers, violent, tough guys.

Lost, he was seething with anger against the city, the whole country, the system that governed his living conditions. He was unable to stop this earthquake, this culture shock, the taste of which remained bitter to him. When he improvised his children's future, he got chills. Uninterrupted questions came to trouble him further. Should he go back to his country to educate them as he wished? Although this was the land of drought, the land from which grass rarely grew, food was scarce, hungry locusts were preying on the little harvest of miles or maize, sorghum or rice.

In his country, the family business was a customary one. There was no judge, no lawyer, and no penitentiary. Often the family usually returned stronger than before. But here, he said, a woman had to open her mouth, crying out for help, and a panoply of ordinary people—psychologists, psychiatrists, police, judges, lawyers—would come to her aid, moving the Sky and the earth to lock up the guilty party.

Erasing his old customs from several generations is like sending him to a re-education camp from where he will abandon his way of living, educating, thinking and acting. Teaching him that this was a life as a couple, when approaching his wife intimately, when intimate approach became a violation of the law. Certainly, it was difficult to undo in a camp what one would have learned in forty years, fifty years. Failure, recidivism would have been commonplace. It would then be necessary to move on to rehabilitation. When he calmed down, he got up slowly, around him, everything turned upside down. He was unable to stand upright, leaning against the tree trunk again. No one spoke to him, he passed unnoticed in the building. Absolute silence reigned in his empty home. He felt exhausted on the bed and burst into tears. Beyond the bitterness, he had to answer for his actions. Who would tell him his rights? Or did he think he had any? Him who constantly cursed the system will confide in a judge? A lawyer?

He went to Daniel's house. In front of the door, a force was holding him, making him take a few steps back. Something was going on inside him. He was certain that his misfortune would be a bad spell that the concierge had cast on him. It was a mistake, but he was thinking of witchcraft, black magic, voodoo, of which he would be one of the adepts. He returned to his house; he went back with a crucified. He walked toward the door, his idea was to eliminate this man, to put him out of his way. As he expected, Daniel opened the door.

"May the peace be with you! Come in."

Valère grabbed Daniel by the collar and kicked the door to shut.

"What peace? Since your arrival, misfortunes have been pouring down on me and you talk to me about peace? You know, old rag, everyone dreams of killing you in this building, me in particular!" (Raising his voice)

"Killing a defenseless old man is proof of cowardice! To be fair, let's say you had to take on a man of your size. Let go of me, I can hardly breathe!"

"I don't care, die! All I care about is making you suffer, depriving you of your life, sending you to the cemetery! That's it, die!"

Daniel was losing his breath, while Valère took the pleasure of dragging him from one room to the other. He stopped in the kitchen, rummaging through the drawers. He took out a large butcher knife and wiped it on Daniel's clothes and continued talking:

"Old people like you have to disappear, you made me suffer. Now that I've got you, you must die, nigger, you look like those who are condemning me to unemployment. Most of them were your age, big mouth, denying me the right to equality, the access to employment! (A burst of laughter). You see this knife sliced, you sharpened it on purpose, knowing your last day of life, eh! And, you didn't even realize that the one who will have the heavy task of sending you in hell is not in this shitty building." (He passed the knife through his head, his neck, his back and then came back on his head. "How about a good surgery on your head? Just to get the hormones out of your big mouth, that make you meddle in the problems of others in this building."

"Get off me, kid! You've already got the cops after you for spousal abuse, you'll get the cops after you for murder!"

"I knew it, I knew you're the traitor among us, die!"

"If you intend to kill me, to end my life, you'll need gloves. You'd have to do something…do something like in the detective movies, leave fewer possible traces, fewer clues. Now, it's too late to commit a perfect murder, you squeeze my throat with your bare hands, your fingerprints remain on my skin. The cops will it pick it like a fruit on a tree, the rest will be dark to imagine, you will not be able to get out of it."

"Stop talking! Don't irritate me, bastard!"

"It's a shame to prefer to abandon your family to live in the shade of the bars."

"I want to kill you! I want to kill you!"

"What do I see in the hand, the crucified? Are you a believer? Crime is the worst of sins. You surely don't want to give up your place in heaven, repent."

"Shut up! I'm sick of your sermons!"

"Then, let go of me! You won't hear me anymore!"

"Out of question! You must die once and for all!"

"Oh, really? I can see that you're scared."

"Shut up! I say shut up!"

"You're just a coward trying to overcome your fear."

"I want to kill you! I want to kill you without mercy!" He choked him; Daniel coughed at the top of his lungs. With an unexpected gesture, Valère was knocked down. Daniel Sahel took pity on this poor man, lost in a universe that was not his own. Despite all the evil he had suffered, he believed Valère was suffering from misery. Poverty had reduced his family to frequently knocking on the doors of charities for food. He tried to distract him, to get him out of his dark thoughts. He wanted to introduce into his mind a new thought, a fact that he would cling to without feeling defeat.

"You have every reason in the world to be angry with me, but you are a good person."

Sprawled on the floor, Valère was torturing himself with abdominal pain, his testicles crushed by the kicks he received from the old Negro, preventing him from standing up properly. He never thought for a second that this old man would be so strong. Little by little, he came back to himself, he turned around, he saw Daniel massaging his throat.

"Where did you learn to defend yourself like that?"

"Here in Montreal, little fool!"

"At your age?"

"Of course, at my age, older people are victims of physical violence perpetrated by fools like you, the newspapers often talk about it. That's twice you've taken me by the throat. The first time I let myself do it because I didn't want to humiliate you in front of your wife and especially in front of your children."

"I thought you were weak!"

"Second mistake, never underestimate a person, no matter what their height or weight. I should have ripped off your testicles completely, I didn't do it out of pity for your wife."

"You almost killed me!"

"Taekwondo! Little fool! An art of peace, a traditional Korean art based on self-respect and respect for others! Beneficial for body and mind!"

"I don't dare believe it, it's violent. Your blows, your screams had destabilized me. You had attacked me without giving me any chance to defend myself, you made me impotent, what will my wife say now that you have taken away the only pleasure she has, her only intimate consolation broken like me, you have left traces. She will bring you to justice!”

“Who is the aggressor?”

“You are! Of course, she’ll accuse you, as well as your bastard Taekwondo sport!”

Daniel Sahel turned Valère’s cries of despair into humor.

“Oh! Poor little asshole! Don’t blame yourself for her, each time she feels like for it, I’ll come and free her from her sexual suffering! And you, like some strange people here, you could always watch us fuck, get some visual pleasure out of it. Ha! Ha! Ha!”

Daniel’s last words made Valère bold again, he stood up, he threw a chair toward Daniel. The old nigger mobilized him for the second time.

“Another advice…stop provoking me, keep the little chance you have left to belong to Anna! I have no indulgence for repeating offences. No matter what you say, I am the victim. Last thing, respect the old people, I urge you to do so. Now, would you please give me a glass of water? My throat is dry…”

Tamed like an animal, he remained in his position for a long time, thinking of the worst humiliations he avoided in front of his family, if a battle took place between him and Daniel in his home. He stared at Daniel and then went to offer him a glass of water. As soon as he drank, Daniel forgot about the treatment he had received. He stood up and coughed several times.

“Valerius! Can I offer you a beer? Or anything else? You look exhausted.”

"Something to eat! I haven't eaten in twenty-four hours."

He offered him some food, a kind of stew with a variety of vegetables. Daniel was heartbroken. A well-built, able-bodied man, with unrecognized intellectual baggage, going around in circles without a job, without a future. How many others around the world are waiting their turn to strengthen the ranks of those who succumb to idleness? One day or another, they will surely land with smiles on their lips, embracing the promised land. They will soon realize that not everything is easy as they imagined it would be. They do not bear the names Bourassa, Tremblay, Bélanger, they will accommodate themselves to the professional steps that would lead them to dead-end roads, to adventure, to abandonment!

Valère saw no light at the end of the tunnel. Reduced to nothing, his troubled thought, affected by humiliation, the pride of a wounded male, he would not have understood the west.

"Big brother! We are in the country of women."

Daniel would not have understood or was he trying to get to the point? Was he referring to his arrest by the police for conjugal violence?

"I would like to point out that this country to my knowledge has always been ruled by men! Where do you get your women's story from? Like all other immigrants here at the United Nations, your problem is a professional one. A man forced to live in charity without the chance to hold office is a dead man. My boy, my little eyes see far, very far! Being a doctor and pushing mops in the hospital corridors is humiliating! Being an engineer and washing dishes in the restaurants is humiliating! Last thing, that's the advice of an old nigger. You have to love women, children, they are everything to society."

Valère got angry.

"Here, they publish our misfortunes, even our most intimate secrets. Everything is a scandal. My own wife humiliates me in front of men! Make me handcuffed like a criminal, throw me in jail? I must restore my honor; I must return her to her own country!"

He hit the table with a punch and then swore. While Daniel helped him to maintain his moral balance.

"Tomorrow is the big day; you will go before the judge. You need a lawyer. They say they have the best vocabulary to convince."

"I will never confide in these men!"

"The game won't be easy."

"I am capable of facing this judge!"

"It is said that they are not always indulgent toward the beaters of women and children."

"So, they should not judge!"

"In front of whom else will you present your arguments?"

"Bah! I don't know, I don't know!"

"You seem to not understand anything, so you'll probably have to call one of your traditional chiefs far away in your native country who doesn't understand any other language than patois."

As Daniel Sahel expected, Valère had no choice. He pleaded not guilty to all the charges, and the judge recommended that he find a lawyer. In the evening, Valère was burning with anxiety. The word guilty was buzzing in his ears, making his lips heavy. He was not the kind of man who could easily dissuade the backward minds that supported the gravity of his actions. He was like a ship on the verge of sinking that had to be rescued, his rudder straightened, his sextant adjusted.

Two days before the hearing, Valère was delirious. He was somehow sitting on a thick cloud that threatened to drop him into hell. He saw himself standing in front of a whole agitated people, making his trial, booing him, throwing stones at him. When he came back to himself, he was sweating profusely, as if he had just come out of a high furnace. Mad with rage, he confessed to God, asking for the easing of his sentence. Far from being satisfied, he constituted by thought, an imaginary court, he believed neutral, impartial, able to render verdicts in his favor. He did not disagree with the idea that the professional environment here was the cause of his decadence. Institutional racism hurt him, his profession was a title without absolute value that anyone could appropriate and claim to be.

Valère attacked him on a few occasions, he blamed himself for having left his native country where he was a person, an executive, a respectable human being with notoriety, living in opulence. He thought he was doing better, having a life beyond the one he was leading in the third world. The happiness that the west made him dream was in fact an illusion, which melted like ice under his feet, letting the current carry him away. The absence of his family at his side caused him a pain of moreover that he wasn't able to contain. No one came forward to share with him this painful suffering. He also attacked his destiny which he hung without a drum, for high betrayal, for having conspired against him, against his family, by imposing alcoholism, smoking, poverty, violence, a life without hope. This fate, even when he was hanged, continued to devastating his life, ridiculing him, turning him into a buffoon.

Valère took walks, he found himself in Jarry Park, swarming with outdoor activities, from where men, women, children, enjoying happiness. He would have liked to be among his own, to pick Nike, to play ball. He slumped on a bench with his hands on his forehead. In his lonely crusade, a man came and sat down beside him. The man took pleasure in feeding the pigeons. He threw bread crumbs into the air, and the hungry pigeons intercepted them in mid-flight. Happy as a king, the man waved Valère by the shoulder.

"It's funny to see all these pigeons fighting in mid-air to catch their food."

Valère replied, "Haven't you ever learned to respect the tranquility of others?"

"Tranquility? But you are in the park, a place to relax. Relax, life is beautiful, sir!"

"Wrong, it is fatal to me! I lost my whole family."

"Oh! What a tragedy! All my condolences."

"They did not die, stupid!"

"How did you lose them all?"

Valère came out of his isolation when he saw the kindness of this stranger, the delicacy of his words, his compassion for him. He told his story, the adventure in which he was plunged.

"May I be on first-name terms with you? My name is Frédéric Roy, my friends call me Fred. I will help you; I am a lawyer."

Valère shivered in the summer heat. Why was the sky so angry with him that it put in his path the people he hated the most? He blamed himself for getting trapped by telling his problem. His silence forced Fred to continue.

"I know how difficult it is to face justice alone, against a well-oiled system. The emotions of what you are going to say, the attacks, the intimidation of the other side etc. There are no gifts to be had in such cases."

"How could you defend me? Correcting my wife is part of my tradition. You know that a tree without a tutor bent."

"You admit that you beat your wife and children."

"Nuance, I don't beat them, I correct them."

"And who corrects you again?"

"Listen to advice of a true man, don't let your woman dominate you, don't let your kids be the boss of parents, you are wrong in this country without traditions, even an animal in the jungle has one."

"What civilization are you from? Here, we passed the animal stage. A woman is equal to a man, we educate children and not bully them, you still live in the Middle Ages."

Valère remained silent, he didn't have to answer that. His strategy was to say to Fred:

"I knew it! You can't defend me. You are inclined toward the feminine cause. I saw how you looking at me and talking badly."

"Should I know everything to better defending you?"

"That's bullshit! I don't trust lawyers, eh! By the way, how did you get to me? The park is large."

"This is where I feed the pigeons. But you don't often visit this park."

"Of course, my children used to come here on the weekends to swing, what do you know?"

"I think I saw your children with your wife, you weren't there. Were you cleaning or preparing dinner during this time?"

Valerie made faces, another indication of what he was afraid of. This time he went further, to find out what might be behind this man.

"You have to understand, Fred, that cleaning and cooking are not appropriate for the man, it's my wife's responsibility. I can't steal it from her anyway."

"As it may displease you, you seem to me to be the kind of macho man, lazy at home, watching television with both feet on the table, while his wife worked to satisfy his four wills."

"You defend my wife too much! Are you in connivance with the Crown Prosecutor? I mean, the one who knocked me out with questions?"

"I am independent, you can confide in me without fear."

A few kilometers away, Anna, his wife had sleepless nights. What troubled her was not the violence in which she lived. She blamed herself for the irreparable damage she did to Valère. What will the family say, her father, her mother, her brothers and sisters, uncles and cousins who stayed behind in the country? What would her husband's family say? By everything, they will hear the echo of her act, they will be indignant, they will condemn her by accustoming her. The day she would set foot in her parents' home would be the last day of her life. She feared revenge, the crime of honor. Any one of these two families could decide her fate. When she thought about how this crime could be, she had goosebumps. In her home town, she could not find help. Had it not been for her presence in Montreal, she would have been a corpse from the first day of Valère's arrest.

Anna met with the police inspector, she asked for a suspension of proceedings, despite everything that was said about Valère's behavior. She was shaking, she was not able to sit down, to hold a long conversation. The inspector turned a deaf ear, he turned the case into a case to be finished.

"Madam, you would say before the judge, all the harm he did to you. You should win this case on behalf of the battered women. He is not a Canadian citizen, if he is found guilty, he will be deported to his country of origin."

She had a frightening panic attack, she was crying, she was beating her chest. She was ready to be reconciled with Valère, if he hadn't seized her parents about it.

"Sir, sending my husband away from this country is like burying me alive!"

In his western mind, it is normal to put an end to a conjugal violence that is perpetuated. Beyond this will, he was unaware that a force remained.

"Madam, your husband will not come back here anymore, you would be safe."

This security that he said was for her an illusion, far from what it would have been for his temerity.

"Sir, have you thought about his children? They will be deprived of their father…I will not be able to set foot in my country again, all my family will abandon me. Even if I stay here, they will send someone to kill me, they will cast evil spells on me. A woman who drives her husband out of the country he drove him to is dead in advance."

The inspector insisted, he was thinking of the intimidation coming from her husband. A death threat, that's what she was subjected to. She would have to realize the seriousness of her miserable living condition.

"Madam, look at your injuries, your husband is a criminal, he will not spare you. You are at the point of no return."

"To my knowledge, he has not killed anyone. The little scratches you see are nothing like the pain my father inflicted on my mother. I still feel lucky compared to what she was going through."

The inspector didn't believe his ears; the revolted woman she was yesterday became submissive, ready to let this man escape to pay for his crimes.

"You are in the west, madam, this barbarism is perhaps minimal for you. But here, it is a serious act. You have chosen to live out of where you come from, respect the laws of this country, abandon your customs."

The inspector had just put all his effort into the water, and Anna carried away:

"Our custom dates back thousands of years, who are you to want to change it?" She burst into tears, hugging her children against her. "They will never forgive me for hurting their father?" She replied.

Meanwhile, Fred was developing a strategy to defend Valère. His behavior, he believed was a function of a deep depression that wasn't treated because of the lack of resources and information available to immigrants. He didn't know how to cope with and which door to knock at. He believed that another cause was the isolation, the lack of work for which he had immigrated for.

Fred improvised a court of law, he asked questions that could well be those of the opposing parties. He called Valère to the bar.

"You used violence causing serious injury to your wife, do you recognize these facts?"

"No."

"You are a man of rare violence, every day you come home drunk, you even annoy the neighbors."

"Do you have any witnesses? They beat me up, threw me to the ground, stripped me naked, humiliated me, handcuffed me like a common criminal. I didn't file a complaint!"

"You tore those words out of my mouth, Valère."

The day of the hearing approached, the fear of just trial in a world he thought was dedicated to women scared him. He thought his lawyer would not be able to help him. Only one thing relieved his state of mind, the fact that he had crucified his fate, opening a new path, he thought. Armed with this little gleam, he presented himself in class accompanied by Fred. When he saw the judge assigned to his case was a woman, the little hope flew away like smoke. That was the great distress. He wondered how to get out of this hurricane? All was lost, all the conditions were there to condemn him, to deprive him of his miserable freedom, to confine him to the shadow of the bars. Standing there, wiping the sweat from his face, staring at the entrance to the courtroom. He thought he saw the woman who was in part the cause of his indictment entering.

As the judge began the hearing, Anna honored him with her absence. It was the crown's turn to panic. The lawyer of the crown asked for time, Fred opposed, the judge granted. The grace period expired; she called the lawyers. While they were debating the postponement of the trial, Anna went home with her children. She wanted by her gesture, to abort the trial, to release her husband of any accusation.

Was Valère right to say his fate was disastrous for him? Was he right to hang him, to crucify him, to put him out of harm's way? Faced with the absence of a main witness, the judge freed Valère from the accusations.

It was euphoria. For the first time, Valère had tender words for judges, lawyers and the judicial system. Now released, he asked that his family be returned to him. His wife, his children, all his human assets, the only wealth he had. He showed up at the address where he was told he could be reunited with his family. He was bitterly surprised when he heard that they had just left for an unknown destination. Valère was depressed again. Head down, Fred dropped him off at his apartment. With the door wide open, Anna cleaned the house, prepared food. Valère thought he was dreaming; he believed it was still his imagination. His eyes reddened with tears, he hugged his children, his wife against him. On the table garnished with cakes, mint tea replaced beer, Valère savored this reunion unimaginable two days ago.

"I understood how precious you are to me; your presence is worth more than all the riches of the world. By the way, how did you get home? I didn't leave the door open."

"Daniel Sahel, he was happy that I came back with the children. He went shopping for the whole family."

"How nice, I will thank him." He went to knock on the door.

"Guess who is there!" He shouted.

"I think I know your voice, before I open the door, solemnly promise me you won't jump on my throat."

Valère burst out laughing.

"I promise!"

With the door open, sitting in the kitchen, Daniel was taking Valère on new paths. He wanted him to go back to school, to learn a new career. Giving up the one he had spent years studying in was the hardest decision he ever made. What is he going to do? He didn't have the Canadian experience that all engineering firms were asking for. He had the responsibility to support his family, to lift them out of the misery, out of the poverty in which he was stuck. He changed chairs and came to cry on Daniel's shoulders.

"My God help me; all my education is no longer worth anything in this country. I was promised all the career facilities with my diploma, I was welcomed here, knowing the trouble I would get into when I left my homeland."

"I understand you, my boy, they promised to all our friends, heaven and earth, that the whole of society would welcome us with open arms, that they would make it easier for us to work once we had touched the ground. We realize that it was all lies and scam."

"Going back to school would be tantamount to approving those who disapprove of our diplomas. How would training here change since we wouldn't always have the Canadian experience?"

Daniel thought for a moment, he was convinced that perseverance in worry would be the only way to carve out a tiny place for himself.

"Do you like to tinker? Go study carpentry."

Valère felt diminished.

"Out of the question, I won't go that low!"

"Yes, you will! You will go, you will find wings that will carry you far, wings that will make all your difficulties a distant memory."

"What would my parents say? That they didn't give me enough baggage to succeed? I'm an academic."

"Like many other immigrants, but they don't want our diplomas, we have to live!"

Valère went back to his apartment, and he was depressed again. After the meal, another discussion, this time with Anna.

"You don't look well; did you argue with the Dean?"

"No, on the contrary, we had talked about work. He suggested that I go back to school to learn another job."

"What do you think about that?"

"I don't know, I have to think about it."

"Daniel is the wise man of the United Nations. He knows what is good and what is bad. He is the one to listen to."

"Have you thought about how people will laugh at me? An engineer who changes jobs for the worse?"

"What's worse? Living in poverty while humiliating oneself or earning an honest living at work?"

"Earning a living from work, the fact that you agree with the Dean convinces me. I will talk to him tomorrow at the first opportunity."

Daniel didn't believe Valère in the morning when he spoke to him about his turnaround. It deserved a cup of mint tea, he said; they sat down in the living room, happy to find solutions for Valère.

"I want your little family to grow and live happily. I don't want anything to keep you in alcoholism and violence anymore. Your success will be the success of all the immigrants who live in your present condition. Do you know? They always say that tomorrow will be better when you live in the abyss. According to the words of a wise old man, tomorrow is not to be waited for, but to be invented…Yes, it must be invented to make better days your own. My grandfather used to tell me: 'When a well is dry, the water doesn't flow anymore. Then, we would have to dig another one, otherwise we would be dying of thirst.' This low life is a sea in which one must swim perpetually, without forgetting the storm that is regularly added to it. Above all, don't forget, no one is better served than by himself."

Valère was attentive to the Dean's words, everything he had lived through when he settled in this country would have left a deep impression on him. He would have liked to see again those who were at the front, this immigration official, who had given him information. He would like to tell him his way of thinking, to call him a liar, a career-breaker. If he could, he would sue him for all the suffering, the pain, the racial Heiner, the poverty into which he was reduced. If he could, he would cry out the injustice with all his voice, so that it could be heard from here in the Maritimes, from here in the Pacific. He did everything he could, he called happiness, happiness was not there. He cried out for misfortune, which plunged his life into the bowels of misery, with no possibility of escaping with dignity.

He took a deep breath, he heard him whispering between his teeth, he had the impression that he was going to camp in his male pride. Suddenly, he abandoned his martyr's face, he became the man he once was. A new man, born of a new resolution. The resolution to go forward, to climb all the mountains, to pass through peaks and precipices. Through this thought, he wanted providence to be his companion, his guide, his success.

Valère subscribed to the theory of the old Dean. He entered school in Montreal to learn new career.

Chapter 6

David walked confidently to meet his friends, carrying a crumpled newspaper that had been dragged ashore by cars. He was trying to straighten the pages, the wind was blowing and carrying away some of the pages. Christ! He cried out before sitting down on a park bench. He had the impression that a treasure was hiding in this old newspaper. He took care to put it in his backpack and waited for the bus.

When he got on the bus, he took out the newspaper and started reading. Turning the pages at random, he came across an announcement that said, "We are looking for labors for various jobs at the Olympic Park." This was the good news he had been waiting for since the letter carriers were back at work.

He got out of the bus and ran toward the workers' lodgings. He was sweating as he climbed the stairs, he was shouting at the door. "Martinez! Martinez, open the door!" He heard the sound of dishes inside, and as soon as he tried to push the door open, it opened. It was Martinez, "To what do I owe this unexpected visit?"

He took the newspaper out of his bag and handed it to Martinez.

"Have you ever read this?" He replied, brandishing it over his head again. Martinez kept a moment of silence, then asked in turn.

"What is this? Another piece of bad news about immigrants?"

Sitting on the stool, he took his glasses and began to read. Suddenly, he cried.

"Work! Work for everyone! Amir, quick! Get dressed before it is gone!"

Amir got up from his seat and came to read the newspaper in his turn. He ran to his room, came back dressed in his costume.

"Let's go! Time is running out!"

Fascinated, his friends stared at him.

"No costume! Especially, no costume!" David said.

Amir had understood nothing, he wanted to be presentable in order to better sell his knowledge, he wondered.

"Why?"

"You are dressed for the work of the bosses! They won't hire you," David repeated.

The atmosphere was tense, the feeling of reliving the work environment without agitation, the joy of having acquired the famous Canadian experience, the second visa as the Dean would say. At the Olympic Park, several people paraded in front of the stuff office. In single file, they waited for the interview. Martinez was called, he shaking on the way to the office. The fear of speaking badly, the fear of to not be hired.

The interview was short in a relaxed atmosphere, he had realized, it was not the welcome he had imagined. The officer asked him:

"I see that you had worked for a numbered company."

"Yes, sir!"

"How long had you worked for this company."

Martinez scratched his head, looking up at the ceiling, looking for answers. He knew that three weeks of experience might not be enough to sell his services. He finally said:

"Less than a month."

"What was your function?"

"Strikebreaker, sir!"

That was too much, the officer burst out laughing and then turned it into a joke. By the way, he never heard such an answer to his questions. Strikebreaker, that's an unofficial position that he could not offer to the candidates. Martinez realized that he had just given birth to his first stupidity, while the officer twisted himself laughing. Martinez was waiting for the verdict with a lot of anxiety.

"What country are you from originally?"

"El Salvador, sir! I am Salvadorian."

"Of course, I don't have the position of strikebreaker here (laughs); however, I need the workers to work during the exhibitions at the stadium. If I accept your application, would you be ready to work tomorrow?"

Martinez was jubilant, he nodded his head in agreement with all the recommendations given to him, but he was especially eager to tell his friends the news. He greeted the officer; at the threshold of the door, he turned around to ask him:

"Sir! I have two friends who want to work."

"And you're going to tell me that they were also scabs?"

Martinez answered again:

"They are scabs, sir! Good workers."

The man couldn't take it anymore, he was dying of laughter.

"Go! Tell them to come and meet me."

He jumped out, signaled to his friends to enter.

"Sit down," said the officer. "Your friend is generous, he is asking me to hire you and I would like to know, are you also scabs?"

Amir and David looked at each other, what trouble had Martinez gotten them into? They were slow to answer, the man continued.

"I hire you all!"

It was astonishment, without an interview, how is that possible? They were thinking of a joke. At the end of all this, Martinez realized that he would be a good actor. He had the audacity to introduce his friends, to save them from the interview.

That rainy Friday brought some good news, and the comrades were urgently called in for a night shift. In the locker room, the indifferent looks of the staff plunged Martinez into the syndrome of the scab worker, he sat down next to his friends. A climate of fear gripped them despite David's presence, and they were eager to begin work. A few minutes passed and the boss came into the room, they got up for work.

Martinez pushed the mop in the area that had been assigned to him, he had to make the place clean for the opening of the event. Learning was child's play, it was easy for him to clean the floor, wash, empty the garbage cans, disinfect the washrooms, and vacuum the red carpet along the visitors' walkway. He worked while singing, he didn't realize that he had just finished his chore. He saw what Daniel Sahel, the old Dean of the United Nations, was saying, like in a movie. Martinez was about to look in the mirror, he burst out laughing. Obviously, he was right about the old African man. What to do now? His work was done according to the rule of art. He went back and forth, combing the work he had done with a fine-tooth comb. He signaled to the manager when he was passing by on his electric vehicle.

"Sir! Mister!"

The boss returned to join him.

"Are you okay? Is everything all right with you?"

"Yes, sir! I'm done, sir!"

The boss were septic, no employee had cleaned this large area in record time. He got out of his electric car and asked him to follow him. They made an inspection. Martinez had the impression that he would be reprimanded if he found things badly done. Without saying a word, they returned to the starting point. What a relief for Martinez, he was waiting for his boss's verdict. This one beckoned to him to get on board his vehicle, he said:

"You're the first to clean this area in a short time, did anyone help you? How could you?"

Martinez had a smile of victory, finally his work appreciated from the first day, he needed more, to beat his record, to prove that he was the best.

"No, sir! I finished it all by myself."

"Good! You are the champion of this place, stay with me."

Martinez let himself be driven by the boss; he watched the others in small areas work hard. A lot of questions were being asked, who is he? He just arrived, how that's possible to parade around with the boss when they were crashing in their chores, swimming in their sweat? The coffee break came quickly, in the staff room all were shooting Martinez with their eyes. The most daring among them spoke to him in a mocking tone:

"Well, well, we'll soon have a new boss!"

It was in this term that Martin Ladouceur expressed himself for the first time. He brought the others out of their silence, giving them the energy to speak out, to revolt against what they call injustice and racial discrimination. What astonished Martinez was the fact that a white man cried out for racism. This language did not fit him, his skin betrayed him, he was far from belonging to the visible minority.

"So, what is he doing among us? There is no place for the boss here!" Bid another standing up, his cup of coffee in hand, staring tirelessly at Martinez.

"Is it a crime against others to do well his and finish it before time?" David eagerly stood up, he expressed himself in this way:

"Listen! That's my friend! He's not a boss!"

"Get away, we didn't ring you!" Martin said more and more angry.

"Is it a fault being a boss? If you're not happy with your situation, look for another job!"

The next day, Martinez found a pile of papers in his locker with messages intended to intimidate him. He could read: "Martinez, your nightmare is just beginning, sign the mouse." He emptied the contents of the locker, he put the pile of papers in the garbage can. The joke continued at lunchtime, when he opened his bag, another message was waiting for him: "Martinez, you are a sewer rat, sign the mouse." He closed his bag, got up, the authors of the messages burst out laughing. Martinez got angry.

"Listen to me carefully! I'm not accusing anyone, but if I catch this mouse writing to me, I'll crush it with my feet!"

Bursts of laughter followed. Martin Ladouceur had just reached his goal. Disturb these immigrants as much as possible, even though there were only four of them. The tone rose, jokes rained down, they were ridiculed for no reason. After he had finished eating, he took a notebook out of his locker and jealously held it in his hand, the harassment continued.

"Do you want to hear the best jokes of the century?" He asked.

"Yes!" His friends replied.

Martinez, Amir, and the other immigrant workers did not expect Martin to specifically target them. The more he talked, the more they realized, their presence was disturbing, aggressive to the point of being hated. Martin Ladouceur asked questions in the form of games.

"How do you call a hated dog?" He looked around at the only black person in the room, winked at his direction. His friends guessed the answer. Some said Haitian, others said hateful.

Martin took great pleasure in hammering on the blacks. He also said that a black and a white man jumped from the fourth floor of a hotel, which of the two would come down first. His friends scratched their heads, the question could have several answers. They guessed, the white one for some, the black one for others. Martin cut off and then died laughing. He said: "The black. Because he is the one carrying the luggage." He continued in the same order and said: "A black man and a white man were flying a plane. After three hours of flight, the plane crashed. The white man, who survived the accident, brought only the black man's head back to the company. Do you know why?" The answer was slow to come, in the rest room, he focused on his comrades with whom he used to play cards. The silence they kept made him understand that he had to give the answer. With smile on his face, he said: "The survivor had to bring back the black box."

This intolerance toward the minority would be the result of ignorance? Born in a small village near Gaspé region, Martin Ladouceur never finished his primary schooling, he had learned by heart the ideas that some people had about immigrants and the lack of knowledge of others. For him, it was natural to mock others, humiliate them, treat them as second-class citizens, discriminate them in short. But one day, when he would become conscious, he would plead ignorance. David did not find this joke funny, as he was the only one who did not laugh. He got up from his chair, went to grab Martin by the collar, stuck his head in an open locker.

"Don't touch my friends anymore! It's pariahs like you who sow racial hatred!"

When he let him go, he made the death. Not another word about immigrants, David went back to get his can of drink. Taking his breath, Martin cried out for vengeance. *Could he still face his comrades? How would he take it?* He chose to obstruct Martinez's work. He was going to taunt him.

"Hey! You'll come and finish my work after yours, where you come from, people work for nothing. Here, you are hard fat, you pay yourself the luxury of the bosses!"

A few minutes later, Jean François ran to meet Martinez in the middle of the corridor, he was scared, he wanted to talk to him. Martinez worried, one moment in this tumultuous environment. He regretted the solidarity between the scabs at Canada Post. He remembered the ransacking, the insults that rained down on them like showers, the pies that were thrown in each other's faces. Frightened by the unknown he had plunged himself into, he thought of only one thing. To keep his little job, to hold on, to show that he was the best. While waiting for the break, he was helping Jean François, then asked him:

"What do you want to tell me?"

"About David, Martin intends to attack him!"

"When?"

"I don't know, but I heard him talking to his friends."

"Thank you, Jean Francois. I will tell him; we will defend him."

"They hate us! For three months that I have been working here, they have not stopped talking against immigrants, about everything that I am black."

"This has intensified with our arrival?"

"Yes! They call you the butter because of your skin tone. If you hear about yellow shoe, yellow or butter, they are talking about you. When they say the word ravioli, they make fun of Séraphino, the Italian. I can't stand the disrespect, the organized racism anymore. Every day, I come to work backward, they don't love us, they want to drive us out of here, to make way for pure wool."

A flash of light went through JF's gray matter, the name his childhood friends gave him. Bad memories came to haunt him, he lived in a village near Petionville. His father was a farmer in the time of Daddy doc François Duvalier. In those days, the ton-tons Macoute came to get some food. They took three or four sheep without paying a cent; he saw his father beaten up every time he opposed to extortion. Being impoverished by papa doc's men, they moved to Port-au-Prince. Reseller of fish at the market, he earned barely two dollars a day, they were crammed into a small house rented at an exorbitant cost. Jean François often slept on an empty stomach. The hurricanes, the repeated storms dispersed the children, JF slipped into the small boat filled with clandestine immigrants heading for Florida. There, he was moonlighting in Haitian circles, collecting enough money to get to the Canadian border. It took him five years to regularize his situation in Canada. As a landed immigrant, his struggle was the same as that of his compatriots. He came back to earth and continued to clean up his area. Suddenly, he saw Martin dumping garbage in the hallways cleaned by Martinez.

The surveillance camera of an exhibitor was filming the scene. Martinez returned to his sector; it was consternation. He ran to find the boss.

"Sir! Somebody dropped off trash in my hallway!"

"Did they? Who could it be?"

"Martin, sir! He's the only one who hates me."

"Are you sure about that?"

"I'll put my hand in the fire, sir!"

"Then get in, come with me and we'll talk to him."

Martin refused to admit his wrongdoing, the manager forced him to join him in a room held by security. He realized that he could not escape, he shouted from afar, forced his boss to turn back.

"I'm sorry Martinez, I messed up your area because your friend called me a brute! I still have a headache. No punishment please, boss, I'll clean up the mess."

Three days of non-stop work, Martinez's effort earned him the title of group leader. This nomination provoked a revolt in the locker room, Martin going to protest at the boss's office. How could he work under the orders of someone he considered inferior? Was this the punishment for obstructing Martinez's work? The boss had a smile, he made him sit down, he asked:

"What can I do for you, Martin?"

"All the staff disapproves your choice of group leader, it's a choice that will have consequences on our motivation to work well in the long term."

"If I understand, you are their spokesperson?"

"Of course, I am!"

"Representing the staff of all races?"

"In fact, whoever keeps silent consents! There was no opposition to what I am telling you!"

"Good! We'll see, accompany me."

In the room, the murmurs gave way to the word of the boss. Standing at the doorway, he spoke in these terms.

"Who are those who mandated Martin to meet with me about the nomination of Martinez? Raise your hands, please."

Martin was in a hurry to raise his, his friends crossed theirs, he felt betrayed.

"But you were with me!"

"Not me!" Amir said.

"Me neither!" David said.

Humiliated, Martin was looking for a way out, he had to show that he was the best candidate unfairly dismissed because of his outspokenness. He did worse.

"Oh my God, explain to me how a stranger who came to my house can tell me what to do? Where to go? Guide me in my daily work? Are we the last of the fools?"

"It's idiots like you who tarnish the names of good citizens, comparing Martinez's work to yours, you don't deserve your job. I won't put a lazy man above the good workers."

Is it too much? The pill was hard to swallow. Martin realized, no one is master in his own home, the reward is based on the fruits of his labor. At work, the new little boss was inspecting behind him with his hands in his pockets. He dragged rags on the electric vehicle that he used to clean and correct imperfections. Suddenly, Martin let go of the mop he was laboriously pushing down the hallway and came to talk to him.

"Listen to me, imported man! Do not come to harass me here! An accident quickly arrived! Do you understand me?"

"Oh! May His Majesty chicken out, I'm doing my job, do yours without grumbling my friend."

"Don't call me your friend!"

"Well, I was to help you and make peace, but I am obliged to ask you to go back to clean the poorly toilet bowls, the forgotten full garbage cans, don't make me report you to the boss."

Angry, Martin released his mop, headed toward Martinez. He took his dentures out of his mouth and threw them at Martinez.

"M…mm…is going to kill you!" He was grinning. His saliva was dripping on his uniform.

Martinez remained calm, he took a glove, picked up the dentures. He contemplated it, he did a forced smile, then kipped it.

"When you want to eat, you will come to me."

"Shut up!"

He showed him the third must, he resumed his work in spite of himself, he had the resentment of the buffalo. *How to get rid of this stranger who was bothering him?*

His eyes darkened by tears; he didn't realize that he had just passed his sector. His friend stopped him:

"You have energy today? You are cleaning my sector; did you finish yours?"

"Damn! Don't tell me I'm cleaning your area."

"Then stop!"

"Of course, I am! Say, I was wondering my God why this stupid butter was born?"

"Who are you talking about?"

"Martinez, look at his skin." (laughing)

"Yellow shoe!"

"It's even better talk to me about it!"

This question has several names, they invented the funniest for the circumstances.

"I heard him chatting the boss, eh! He is crazy! He made me vacuum the carpet to the rope, he calls it the perfection."

They saw him from afar, everyone had their heads down, pretending to pick up garbage stuck to the carpet. Martinez braked in front of them, Martin whispered quietly.

"To walk the ass on this car, life is beautiful, tabarwette!"

"Amigo! It should rather be said in Ostie! Have you forgotten?"

"Are you making fun of us?"

"I give you back your teeth, amigo! I tried to sell them, but nobody wants them, even the city museums."

Martinez, the beast, Martinez, the madman, Martinez, the butter, only nicknames for a man who wanted nothing but to work honestly, to earn a living by the sweat of his brow.

Martin did not learn any lessons from his boiling behavior, inconsolable, he only had in mind the word revenge, without considering the consequences. He ran into the rest room, took a jar of vaseline from his locker. When Martinez left his eclectic vehicle for inspection in other areas, he quickly came to spread the petroleum jelly on the vehicle seat. He returned to his workplace happy with his misdeeds.

Martinez got on the vehicle, stained his pants with oil. In the rest room, everyone burst out laughing. *How did it happen*? They wondered. The culprit turned his back and wiped his hands without saying a word.

The exhibition ended ten days later, they had to pack up. They have to go to the labor center, run around the city looking for new jobs.

Staying at home without work was a heavy burden for Amir. He could no longer sleep, the task of taking care of himself was colossal without a family. Nostalgia for the happy days in the family, the bustle of the city where he was born, everything came back to haunt him in force, taking him away like a flood he could not get out of.

In the night that followed his worries, Amir had a nightmare, he saw himself caught under fire at the demarcation line. He was sneaking through the ruins, and a hole in a pile of concrete provided him shelter. His heart was beating incessantly, he crouched in a corner waiting for a calm. Heavy weapon fire was deafening him, he covering his ears. A few minutes passed and he stuck his head out, looked from left to right; he decided to continue on his way to the family residence. In front of him, snipers unloaded their machine gunners on a stray dog, his belly on the ground, sliding under a half-burned truck. There, he witnessed the exchange of heavy weapons between the belligerents. Amir, in turn, threw a stone in the direction of the path he was to take, and as soon as he moved away, the truck was pulverized. He slipped again between two concrete blocks, and from there he watched the militiamen shoot down two unarmed opponents at point-blank range. This awful scene made him think that he would be the next victim if he did not manage to rejoin his family. Amir had tears in his eyes, his head covered with dust from the force of the shot.

No path was safe, he reached an alleyway closed by the demolition of a large building; he picked up a fully loaded assault gun on the ground. A little further on, lay the body of a naked man, his genital organ torn out, his shoes stolen, he was in a state of advanced decomposition.

Amir blocked his nose, he was crossing an unfenced courtyard, dragging his weapon with him. Will he use it against an assailant? He had no idea how to handle the weapon; it was used as bait; he could be shot without warning; he could scare off those who were unarmed.

Amir decided to try his weapon, kneeling on the ground several shots went off without waiting, provoking a serial reaction from the fighters. He tried again; his weapon made him jump backward. It was hard to learn in a besieged city. He had to cross this murderous line, how to do it without getting shot? He fired a burst in a direction opposite to his route, he crossed the line in a rain of fire. The more it was, the more he would leave his skin. Amir stormed into a deserted residence, his gun in firing position. He saw a radio set on the table, turned it on, and heard the worst news. The Israeli bombardments of Palestinian positions, the reinforcement of the Syrian armed forces in Beirut, the hostage-taking, the clashes between the different militias, the massacre of Sabra and Chatila—this apocalypse made him disgusted with life. But before dying, he had to reach the family residence. Hungry, he ate the pieces of dry bread he picked up from the kitchen floor. He turned on the tap, not a drop of water, opened a door to a room, and discovered three bodies riddled with bullets. Behind him, a ten-year-old boy who had been trapped between the bodies was crying out for help. Frightened, Amir hid himself. He saw the boy and came to get him out of his hiding place.

"What are you doing here?"

"I escaped the carnage!" The boy replied, still traumatized, shaking all over his body, his teeth chattering like the bell tower of a church.

"Where have they gone?"

"I don't know, they are beasts! Not humans." He burst into tears.

The boy told him in detail about the horror he had experienced: "There were several of them, they tied my father, they raped my sister and my mother in front of my father before killing them with bullets on their necks. They had looted everything of value, destroyed what they couldn't take away. I was cowardly witnessing this carnage without intervening; I could have killed at least one of them before I died. I blame myself! I am a coward!"

His tears flowed like a fountain, Amir dropped his weapon, he took the boy and held him close.

"You are brave! You have to live to tell all these horrors! Let's go away, we are in danger."

The boy refused to leave, he preferred to die there, next to his family.

"Hey! Will you abandon yours? They are my parents! I am their guardian."

"Guardian of the corpses? You're unarmed, how will you defend them? Stop being stubborn and follow me! We will try to get out of this hell without borders. You know I'm not sure if I'll find mine alive."

House by house, they arrived a few meters from the family residence; Amir in turn witnessed the massacre of his parents. Men ran out with precious objects in their hands and lay on the floor. A few seconds later, the house collapsed under a cloud of dust. How could one not react to such a massacre? The boy threw stones at them, he was shot down; Amir was captured. In the night, he took advantage of the fighters' deep sleeps to escape. Alone in this cruel world without pity, how could he escape? He ran without knowing where his legs were leading him, at the crossroads of the street, he ran into an Israeli army tank. He thought he was coming out of the mouth of the wolf and into the mouth of the lion. Once again, a captive, he was released for his age, and continued to walk along the way to the refugee camp. Amir awoke from his sleep, he trembled as if he was in the combat zone. Outside, he picked up the mail that the letter carrier had left in the box. Suddenly, he shouted a cry of joy. He had just received a letter from Lebanon. He tore the envelope, his hands were shaking, he plunged into the reading.

"Dear, nephew, I hope this letter finds you in good health, like many Lebanese, you probably thought I was dead, buried. I survived the blasting of the family home. Don't worry, I thought you were dead too. How happy I was when I learned that you were safe in Canada. Without delay, I approached Myriam's parents so that you could marry her. Is life beautiful where you are? I hope you are not married. Take care of yourself, answer us as soon as you receive this letter."

Amir cried again, marrying Myriam would be the most beautiful thing in his life. He was gloating, he momentarily forgot the headaches he was lamenting.

This letter had the effect of a rebirth of a new life. He put on his music, he started to dance.

"Finding a person, you love and then you thought was dead deserves a great celebration" Martinez suggested.

"Not only is he alive, he's courting for me the most beautiful girl in the country, she's the kind of woman that the men in our country love."

"She's beautiful like who?" Martinez asked.

"She's a perfect creature without equal."

"Hey, Amigo, don't lose your head. All women are the same."

"I have to answer right now before it's stolen!"

"Are you kidding me!"

"No! In Lebanon, you have to expect everything. Someone would give all his fortune to have a woman more beautiful than the goddess."

Amir replied to his uncle, he was a new man, a happy man who brought out his feelings toward both the family and the woman he coveted. He described his life in Canada as an unexpected opportunity, a paradise he was eager to share with his loved ones. He dreamed of making a home away from home. Shells, cannon fire, and constant bombing that he barely knew for a year.

Finally, he was happy to find the future woman of his life, the second letter he received from her was devastating. A long list of the dead reminded him of the continuing bloody inside Beirut. The horror of the massacres sent shivers down his throat; his hair rose up. Photo of Myriam he received came to moralize him, to give sense to his life. He abandoned the letter for a moment, took the photo, and began to dance, to shout, to express the joy. The question that came to his mind was how could she survive from the rapes, the kidnappings and the blind bombardments of Beirut?

He read this letter that shocked and comforted him at the same time. "Hello, you! I don't know when you will receive this letter, I will be still alive here in Beirut, things are going badly. I am writing to you from underground, under the bombings of the Israeli air force. I would like to share with you, happiness, even if it is mired in misfortune with no country and no future. I am writing to you under the fire that brings down what remains of the ruins that could shelter the refugees. What can I say about the rockets that shake us at every moment, what can I say about these women, these children, these old men murdered in their sleep? The list of the holocaust is long, hold your breath. Your uncle is no more, he was a victim of the fanatical fighters who sow terror in the ruins. We buried him under the gusts of sniper fire, there is no respect, not even for the dead.

Subjected to blackmail by weapons at the wrists, one is reduced to nothing, my chances, my hopes, are constantly murdered, death is shown to me as a way to freedom. No one hears my voice, lost in the cries of distress, stifled by the tireless raids of gunfire in Beirut. Through this war, I lead my own struggle; that of holding on to life, to make it harder for me in all this suffering. I face the people who would like to push me further into the pit, those people who ruthlessly attack the peacekeeping force, thinking they would go straight to heaven.

I would like to write you pages and pages of love and romance, I would like to think only of you, since the first letter that gave me the taste of life. But the insecurity, the dangers that await me divert my mind. I am writing to you with my ears closed, watching the militiamen shoot men stripped of their belongings. Neither law nor faith can stop their impulses. How can we get out of this hell? How to leave this Fireland? Dad will try this month to lead us to Egypt, by what miracle, I don't know, will we reach our destination? I don't know either.

Whatever happens, know that I love you. I will wait for you all my life; I will know how to protect myself against everything that can unfortunate me…Well, my candle is going out, darkness and fear are starting to take their toll on me. I will imagine a quiet night far from Beirut from where the Israeli air force has just dropped a ton of bombs. There are many culprits, you know them, I can't name them for the fear of reprisals."

A disturbing story that drove Amir crazy. He was thinking how to get Myriam out of this hell. How could he have peace of mind when the woman he loved was in danger? Crossing Lebanon for exile would not be an easy thing, he knew too much, he almost left his skin on many occasions. He resented the instigators of these interminable conflicts that had thrown him on the pavement.

"Have faith, Amigo! She will come out of it just like you." Martinez said.

"These terrorists attack everyone, they did not spare the peacekeeping force!"

"No, Amir! Word of amigo. She will come out unscathed from all these operations I swear on Santa Maria!"

For two months that Amir had been waiting for news of Myriam, what has she become? This long silence worried him more. In the afternoon, the post deposited a letter coming from Egypt. Amir was finally assured that Myriam was safe, he plunged back into reading.

"Dearest hope, if I've held out so far, it's because of you! I love you. The strength of my love for you fights alone against all those men who brandished their weapons on us. Dad was to negotiate our departure to the gang that held our corner of the ruins. He was almost assassinated several times. Subjected to interminable interrogations, he was taken for a traitor, here how he told us about. A few meters from the headquarters of the armed group, a masked man told me to raise my hands up. I did what he asked me, I advanced in his direction. One of them came out of a hiding place, put a black hood over my head and dragged me into a hole I don't know where they drove me. They warned me not to try to escape, as I would risk jumping on the mines nearby.

Hours and hours of anguish drove me crazy, when they came back, they shoved me, they locked me in the trunk of the car. I didn't know where they were taking me, what would they do to me? When I got out of the trunk, they asked me to shut up, the chief would decide my treatment. In a large, well-guarded room, I had a beautiful view, I thought the worst. They were making me see beautiful things before killing me? In fact, this was my last wish. The moment of interrogation came, the machine gun stuck to my neck, I had to answer the questionnaires, even if it was impertinent.

'Who are you?' The chief asked in a deep voice. I trembled with all my old bones. He didn't care about my marital status, he wanted to know what I was doing in his area of influence.

I would like to have some protection in order to get my family out of here. The man burst out laughing and then grabbed me by the glue on my shirt. He kicked me brutally, I felt at his feet.

'Why would you want to get out of Beirut!'

We are in danger, stuck in the basement; we risk dying of starvation. It is better to leave now that there is a lull. The man got angry, he grabbed me again, he spat in my face.

The vast majority of the remaining population is not human. Your skin is worth more than ours.

I was hit on the head, lying on the ground, I couldn't get up. Two of the armed men lifted me up, I could not stand on my legs. They made me sit down, I could hardly breathe. I began to asphyxiate and one of the men took the hood off my head. The head of the sector disapproved of this humanitarian gesture and came to hand it to me with such brutality that my nose was bleeding.

'Let him die! He will not spare us when peace comes! He came in peace; he needs our help!'

'Out of the question, kill him! He has seen our faces!'

I saw the death coming to smell me, I clung on in terror when the fighter made me get up from the piece of concrete that served as a stool. I was walking in the footsteps of a man whose soul would soon be free from his body. My wishes were to see my daughter Myriam again, to kiss her, to say goodbye before I died. I got back in the car, I didn't know which direction he was taking, would it be the cemetery? An ideal place to get rid of me once I was murdered.

I prayed inside in silence that all those whom I unintentionally offended would forgive me, so that God would have my soul. When the car stopped, I thought this that's it, I was expecting to be decapitated. I imagined them riddled with bullets, an atrocious death that I wouldn't have wished on anyone, even my captors. Already ten minutes after the car stopped, I couldn't hear a sound. With my hands tied, I could not remove the hood that was hiding my face. Suddenly, voices were heard, people were bargaining with me, they could not agree on the amount to claim from me. The hope of getting out of the decline was beginning to be born in me, I remained confident. They walked toward me, they took off their hoods and pointed their weapons at me.

'Listen, grandfather, we had given values to your carcass!'

'What do you mean brave fighters?'

They looked at each other and laughed. One of them pulled out a pistol and pointed it at my forehead.

'All your fortune against your freedom, grandfather!'

I held my breath, I weighed my words, there was no way I would let myself be shot down. They ordered me to look them in the face, they wanted my reaction.

'I am not very wealthy, my children, but you can dispose of my property.'

'Give up your grandfather's life, your property is in ruins!'

'Please! Let me and my family out of this hell!'

They spit in my face again they kicked me. Spread out on the piles of pieces of concrete, I had difficulty getting up.

'If we understand well, grandfather, your skin is worth more than ours. Is that really the reason for your presence in this forbidden zone?'

I was given the hood; I regretted my recklessness. I should have stayed under the ruins with my people. They locked me up for four hours and then transferred me to another place as ruined as the previous one. There, the boss recognized me, he gave me the famous, "Salam Alaikum" greeting before asking me:

'Is the safety of your family the only reason for you to leave the place?'

'Yes,' I replied. He stared at me, he added.

'You are all a coward! You refuse to die as heroes and martyrs.'

'What help would a frail old man give you? I will burden you more than help, let us go, please...'

'If we are talking about money, how much will you pay to save your rotten skin? A million? Two million?'

'Give me the assurance to leave before we talk about money. You are a smart man,' he answered, 'I will not promise to ensure your safety beyond our zone of influence. However, I have a friend, today we don't get along because off our political allegiances, nevertheless we have respect for each other.'

He took a piece of paper from his pocket and tore it in half. He wrote a few words, a pass. That's how we got out of hell."

What a relief for Amir, finally he could breathe, he could hope that one day, he would take Myriam in his arms, cover her with a kiss, tell her that she is his whole life.

A week after, a man was sitting, wearing a blue coat. The man seemed to be scrutinizing everything around him. Crouching on his knees, he had been there for several hours. The curious neighbors wondered if he was a newcomer. It was the lady who thought she saw the immigrants landing like butterflies flying over the old girls. She urged her neighbor to get out, describing the youngster as an animal seeking refuge in the bad weather. Her neighbor's response was slow. She got up from her old chair and went to look out the window. Naked, Catherine jumped on the old Dean who was forcing himself to give her orgasm. She was in a state of trance. Suddenly, her cry was followed by tears of joy. Hands to her face, she gently backed away, she took care not to be seen. "She took me for a bitch, while I trusted her. I'm the last of the bitches!" She came out of her house to match her gossip, she made a wink at the him.

She went down the stairs, she approached him. "Handsome, it's annoying to stay like this all alone, nailed to the ground. Get up, come and quench your thirst." At the apartment, Catherine closed the curtains on the windows, unplugged the phone. She came to sit on the chair, showing her bare chest from time to time, her partially dry legs, opened up and her pink panties could be seen. A little silence reigned and then she decided to start the conversation. "What's your name?" In a soft voice, the man replied, "Samuel, my name is Samuel, my friends call me Sam," she winked and then took a small book from the table. "Sam as Uncle Sam of the Americans, right? I love that name," she gave herself excuses to approach him, sometimes she put her hair back on, sometimes she wiped a small stain on the shirt, holding a glass of beer in her hand. Catherine poured the contents of the glass over Sam and ran to get a towel. "I'm sorry," she said, "I'm so embarrassed. I won't let you go out with that body odor, come on! Take your shower, I'll wash your clothes." Sam was trapped, he didn't have a change of clothes, he rolled up a large towel when he came out of the shower. "Come into the room, I'm waiting for a delivery, I don't want you to be found in this situation. Lie down, rest while you wait for your clothes."

A few moments later, she got naked, she slipped into bed, she stuck herself against him. Sam turned his back, and with one hand, she grabbed his genitals. She was pulling it, she manipulating it and it became hard. Sam resisted, he said: "Madam, let go of my stick, you're going to tear it off." She burst out laughing, she tickled him everywhere, she kissed him sensually, stopping him from speaking. When she detached her lips from his, Sam made her understand: "It's called rape, madam, I didn't give you my consent!" She took a long breath and then she made him understand. "What, rape? I'm a hot widow, I forgot my vagina years ago. It no longer speaks to me; I had deprived it of its divine pleasure. I have to give him his present, let it be, you won't regret anything, young man." She took off her dentures, she pushed the penis down to the throat. She treated it; its substance overflowed from her mouth. "That's it! I'm ready, get in my vagina." She rode over him, he grabbed her firmly, she launched her cry of pleasure. She held him, she seemed to share the orgasm with all her cells.

"Uncle Sam, this is our secret, no one has to know," she said.

"I'm all yours, here, take my phone number, I want to have a suite." Sam got his clothes; she took him out the back of the house. Samuel went for a walk in the area while waiting for his friend to arrive. During this time, Catherine knocked at Ellen's door.

She said, "Ellen! Ellen! Why aren't you answering?" Ellen was talking to him from a distance. "What do you want? I'm relaxing, I'm over the moon." Catherine raised her eyebrows. "Since when have you been over the moon? Get out of bed, your coffee will get cold!" They sat down around the table; Catherine continued. "Was it long? Was it short? I don't doubt it; especially since I saw you at work, naked, on horseback. You let yourself go, you jumped, you made a deep cry before collapsing on his chest." Ellen couldn't believe her ears, how had she guessed all that?

She laughed loudly. "How long have you been spying on me?" Cathy smiled broadly. "It's by chance, my dear, I wanted to introduce you to a beautiful bull from nowhere!" Ellen nodded sadly, she replied, "I wish you had tied him to a pole."

The appetite comes by looking at his anatomy. She refused to tell him that she owns this bull, nor where he comes from, where he is going. Suddenly, the secrets came out.

"You let him go without introducing him to me!"

"You're a real bitch, I thought you were spotless! While you have discreet relations with this old nigger who hangs around here and there. Was this old nigger your first prey?"

"All good women are entitled to his secret garden; I can't reveal it for fear of losing him."

Catherine made a grimace, she went back to sit on her rocking chair, her eyes fixed on the sky. She was thinking of the time she had wasted chatting since she had met her neighbor, who was enjoying herself in the privacy of her own home.

Across the street, Samuel found the Dean in great shape with his friends. Excited like a child who had just received a toy, he was boasting of his exploit.

"The feminine warmth is intense in your corner."

The Dean turned around toward the door and suddenly stood up as if he had lost something.

"Clarify your thought, young man!"

"Ah! Here comes one who knows too much." (Laughter)

"Get to the point! Spare us from your nonsense," the frustrated Dean resumed.

"I've just had my lunch with your neighbor."

"But they are old for your age!" The Dean said.

"I know! And it's in the old cauldron that you can find good sauces!"

"Which one has lunched you? Ellen? Catherine? They're widows!"

"And since they have no right to pleasure, their dead husbands will come back to haunt them tonight."

Daniel (The Dean) was overcome, he didn't believe for a moment that these women of his generation could let themselves be tempted by youth. The anxiety and fear of losing his hidden treasure visibly affected him. He, who had the art of flirting with women of his own age, did not accept Sam's presence in his backyard. He warned him.

"Don't try to make ladies your object. What would your young wife say if she found out about this? Polygamy is forbidden in this country."

"Listen, old fox, I was just passing through your neighborhood. Don't blame me, this woman asked me to put an end to her sexual suffering. I see that there is a desperate need for strong men in your kingdom."

Daniel shot Samuel with his eyes. Ellen was his confidence; he had no idea that she would fall into the arms of another, when he had just left her. He went to knock on the door, waited a long time, and concluded that there was no one inside. At the main entrance, Daniel heard a voice similar to Ellen's. He went to the door and waited for a long time, concluding that there was no one inside. Reassured, he rushed up the few steps, leaning on his cane. "Ellen! Ellen!" He shouted. She was in the company of a man holding her by the waist. He was her cousin; she hadn't seen him for several months. The man gave her a kiss, he greeted Daniel and left the house. Ellen was surprised that Daniel was coming back so soon to see her. He looked angry and confused. He had only been trying to preserve what he had gained for an hour, but the intrusion of the second man made him lose hope.

"Who is this guy? He put his arm around you!"

Ellen was amused, she stroked him on the back, Daniel continued to ask questions.

"Come and sit down for a while," she suggested.

"Not until you tell me who this guy is!"

"He's my cousin!"

"He was flirting with you! He gave you kisses! Two men in less than an hour, is that a disease?"

"Two men, where did the second one come from?"

"Samuel! He's going everywhere to tell about his adventure."

"I'm not interested in him, he's too young for me! I see what you mean, this boy was in company with Catherine. I never met him, she was looking for him in front of the door of the young men across the street, the new immigrants you know so well to go often to their homes. Daniel! Our relationship is no longer discreet; Catherine now knows everything about both of us. She saw us through the window making love, we had indirectly triggered the cessation of her abstinence. She is angry with me for hiding everything from her, even though she used me as an example of a widow faithful to her late husband." (Holy widow)

Daniel listened attentively to Ellen's story, nodding his head whenever his interest was defended. He deflated like a balloon when she offered to formalize their relationship. It was a legal way to satisfy his baser instincts in plain sight. Ellen had a guilty conscience for her lifelong friend; Catherine would kill her for treason. She lived without affection, neglected by her own people, and no one asked about her. Happiness had been keeping her company ever since she swore to follow in Cathy's footsteps. She took Cathy's trifles for granted, she was her voice and her ears, she brought her all the neighborhood news. Moved, all these stories reminded Daniel of the difficulties to come. He hugged Ellen tightly and they hugged for a while. Ellen had grown children, grandchildren. They came every Sunday for family dinner. Daniel's phobia was the reaction these children would have, one of whom was a cop, known for beating up immigrants at a demonstration downtown. Ellen's beautiful words didn't reassure him, his nervousness was visible, his hands trembled when he wanted to express himself. He had to react, he had to say something.

"Ellen, what will your children think? That you fell on your head? Old negroes like me, not everyone would like to have a friend or cousin in this society. I'll be a source of unimaginable problems for you. Your broken promise, that of a faithful widow's home, alone will cause an upheaval in our relationship."

Love has no age, love is a phenomenon that characterizes men, women, young and old. It is like the wind that blows, carrying away in its path the hearts it wishes to please. It can make some jealous, others happy. It can break hearts like the lightning that tears the sky, making all feelings and affection disappear in a single gesture. Often ungrateful, to leave many in endless depression, often cruel to provoke duels, incidents leading to murder. Revenge in disappointment is one of his actions, what to say about the suicides of all those humans for whom he constitutes for them, the air they breathe, the balance, physical and mental, without which they would cease to evolve in society.

Daniel Sahel had the impression that he had just made swallow this phenomenon to the only woman who avidly desired it without any criteria. Once he had tasted the water from her fountain, he believed that she would ask for it again since she would always be thirsty. Who would have thought that this Dean of nickname, this old fool, so to speak, would persevere several years to fall into the arms of the woman who, well married, made the men wet their panties when she passed by? Was it her clothes? Her size? Her sexual steps, giving the impression that her whole body was dancing to the rhythm of her steps? Frozen in his long reflection of love, he forgot that he was still in the middle of a conversation.

"Listen, Daniel, there are only fools who don't change their mind. I didn't betray anyone, my promise dates back to when my children were young. I didn't want a man other than their father to set foot in the house, I wanted them to grow up in a healthy environment, I didn't want anyone to be able to say that I abandoned them for a husband. Today, they are grown up, each one has founded his own home, they work, they are self-sufficient."

Was Daniel to believe in this mystical union that she naively believed without repercussions of any kind? Could she bear the heavy task of explaining to her friends and relatives that the man she dreamed of after the deceased husband had finally emerged in her heart? Would she know how to dispel from the worldly eyes of Daniel's presence. The first person to be tamed was Catherine, she lived in the immense distress of a widow who, as the years went by, realized too late that she had not taken into consideration the bogging down of her feelings in fidelity outside of love. Looking a man in the eye, wanting him would not have been her strong point without Ellen's consent. The bridge was broken, it remained to be rebuilt.

While walking in Jarry Park, Ellen's head was heavy with thoughts. Catherine thought she had just broken up with her old African nigger. She took a few steps and then stopped with her head down.

"Ellen! Ellen! Wake up! Wake up! I feel like you've sold your soul to this nigger man, you're not the Ellen I know anymore! A cheerful, humorous, lively woman who sent men on their way."

Catherine was certain that this time she would convince her neighbor to end the relationship that was only meant to keep them away from each other. How could she give up the pleasures of being together on the balcony in the heat of summer, laughing at men, provoking others with the sole aim of creating leisure for themselves?

How can an old friend let herself be tormented by the sex of a man who couldn't stand up straight without his stick? She imagined the work Ellen would have to do to keep upright and light her half-defective lighter, whose flame could barely warm the immense pleasure she expected to enjoy.

Love is ungrateful to her in regard to friendship, in fact, it is also comparable to a disease, an epidemic that inhabits each individual whose awakening wreaks devastating, collateral victims who could not escape without after-effects.

Could Catherine defeat this scourge that even the strongest households succumb before it like poisoned rats, leaving entire families broken, disoriented, divided, unhappy children, drawn from left to right, without the slightest pity?

His certainty quickly turned into a nightmare when his girlfriend smiled a little smile on the corner of her lip. She continued walking without saying a word. Quickly, her behavior frustrated Catherine, she did not know how to approach her. Was it the discovery of her sentimental secret that was torturing her? She searched for reasons without success. In the noise of the pigeons' flights, from which a whirlwind of wings spread out above them, this love brought Ellen out of her silence. Bewitched, her spirit was absent when Catherine asked herself questions inside. She knew that her answers would disappoint her, she didn't have the magic words to put on the table as a gift to unwrap. Pushed by the energy within her, love as fresh as the winter wind, she believed that the time was right to share her pleasure, although she would not have been forced to do so. What would Catherine's reaction be? A congratulation? An encouragement to have finally fallen into the arm of a predator who hadn't stopped admiring her, to have been hovering around her for years without really getting close to her? She thought she deserved hugs for this feat, she who was by nature shy, unable to look up in front of a man. That day, she devastated her gossip, reducing it to dust.

"Cathy, I did not sell my soul as you seem to believe! There is a new entity grafted into me, it controls all my feelings, my tastes, my pleasures, my passions. It awakened in me the sleeping love, the joy of living. This entity changed my life, it gave me the hope that I would no longer think of going six feet underground. Open your eyes, look at me. I am back to being the woman I was. Beautiful ebony hair, better makeup, I found orgasm, joy of life, to let myself be pampered like a child. Don't you miss all this? You're not old, your life is not over, you have to reinvent it, fill it with passions, make it live with one of those entities that make love emerge!"

Catherine was startled, she was reviewing the scene with precision when she went to knock on the window. The passion Ellen had for Daniel, the cries of pleasure that overpowered her, her claws that held the sheets and the tons of waves that he dumped would have been no stranger to her new way of perceiving things. These abundant pleasures are a trap for old ladies.

"I can see you bewitched by his spray gun! Listen, Ellen, we forget about everything, we come back as before."

Catherine did not understand that her gossip had invited her to remedy her life as a Hermit. She still thought she could make Ellen change, bring her back to her front corner, get rid of the old nigger.

Ellen would not have been as easy as she thought. What she heard could upset her, she could hardly recover.

"I confess that this old nigger, as you called him, has been my courtesan for many years. Now I wish only one thing, to take him as my husband!"

Cathy slumped on the bench. She thought that at that age, they supposed to have the rosaries in their hands, kneeling in front of St Joseph's Oratory, climbing the steps to the top from where, crying over Brother André's grave, they would ask God for forgiveness. Cathy was already thinking about how she could turn Ellen away from breaking the bridges that linked her to this endless adventure, which endangered their friendship.

"Marriage at your age? It's madness! (Laughter) Your children will give her a hard time! It won't last more than half a moon. (Laughter) Listen, Ellen, you were a slave to your late husband, working day and night to satisfy his every whim and those of your children. You slept last, woke up first to offer breakfast. You washed and ironed the clothes of the whole family; you swept and cleaned the house. Meanwhile, the man, with his feet on the chair, would block out the slightest noise because he was listening to his hockey game. As soon as you got out of that prison, you were ready to go back in. This time, to wipe who? A nigger! A slave rehabilitated in society; he's trying to equalize our men by taking you in his arms. How will you see him at night? He's black!"

That was too much! They were tearing each other apart in the park, to the gaze of the young men who were lingering to leave in front of such a spectacle. What interested these young people was not only their cries, their disarray. Much more their ages. They hadn't believed that these ladies could still squabble over the love of a destitute old Negro, when love doesn't know the age factor?

Ellen slapped Cathy, she didn't like her vulgar language, she tore the scarf from her head. They hurled insults at each other in front of this crowd of young people. They stopped playing soccer, they watched two old chickens who no longer melt, fighting.

Here was a first chapter that turned to vinegar, Catherine had tears in her eyes. Alone on the way back, her steps weighed on her, one would have thought she was climbing a mountain, that she was carrying the burden of humanity. She looked at all the possibilities of diverting her best friend, her lifelong girlfriend, to the path they had taken before. The great obstacle, the great culprit was none other than love, it is she who strikes, annihilates, takes everything in his path. Could she face him? Could she tell him what she thinks? The insults that she dedicated to him? She believed for a moment in an unleashed curse, sent by this African sorcerer, a spell that was cast on Ellen that she would have to get rid of at all costs, call on the parish priest. What exactly should I tell him? That her friend was possessed by evil force? What sign? What symptom could attest to what she is saying? She suddenly got up from her chair and opened the fridge. She took a bottle of vodka; she poured a glass into a glass and drank it in one go. She lay down on her bed, turned and turned around.

The two hours of sleep she had did not calm her ardor. She thought she could exterminate this love on her own. She meditated on the means; she was going around in circles in her house without knowing what weapon to use. While she was racking her brains, Ellen was the happiest widow in the neighborhood. On Friday evening, she wore the most beautiful of her dresses, she had put on make-up, her silhouette compared to that of the legendary Barbie, and once again made Daniel Sahel lose his head. Was it to make up for his youth lost in time? The time she devoted to her home without worrying about leisure activities, the joy of being with friends, the pleasure of being in the arms of a young man, crossing together the threshold of the door leading to the ballroom?

Ellen had chosen a nightclub frequented by young people. At the entrance, the security guard made them wait; he had the impression that the couple was in the wrong place, he inquired inside, he came back to tell them:

"Grandpa, you are not allowed here!"

Daniel Sahel did not understand this decision, yet this club was a public place with no age restriction. He demanded and obtained the intervention of the manager. Once inside, they noticed that everyone was staring at them. When the music was playing, he said to his girlfriend:

"Let's go! Let's go! Dance is the best sport! They are looking at us, don't be embarrassed! We're going to excel the pace, develop our potential! Show these young people that we are better than they are!"

Shyly, she let herself swing to the rhythm of the music. This dance they did was different from the one they did today. All eyes were fixed on them. Distant memories came to materialize as they emerged within this couple, dancing was as much a pleasure as having a drink while eating a good meal. No matter what these young people around them thought, they had somehow brought a forgotten spicy item from the old drawer.

Ellen was sticking to him, she regained her strength, her passions in this new atmosphere, not very welcoming, full of emotions. Suddenly, curiosity gave way to admiration. A very courteous young man presented himself at their table:

"Madam! Madam! Sir! Would you allow me to sit down for a moment?"

Daniel was suspicious at first sight, *could it be a trap? A drug dealer? Why would he be interested in an old couple looking for pleasure?* Ellen grabbed him by the shoulder, he nodded. The man sat down, ordered them a drink. This gesture although friendly irritated Daniel, he wondered inwardly to what honor this kindness is worth to him? The man remained smiling, took a sip from his glass and then began to speak:

"I've been going to this place for years; I've never seen a couple as dynamic as you! You laze younger than us, do you live on the water of youth? Please excuse my recklessness? Would you grant me a dance with your nice lady?"

Daniel hesitated, he kept silent and seemed to say no. He thought that having a woman who is the envy of young people is proof of the radiant beauty of his companion. Was she ready to change riders? Would she have to consent to it? In his old days, the word belonged to the husband, absolute master of his destiny, but this era being devolved did not allow Daniel Sahel to decide this. He ended up answering him:

"If it pleases madam to grant it to you, I am well at ease."

Ellen was overjoyed; for the first time that such an honor was reserved for her. Her life as a housewife was changing day by day, to rise above her hopes. Of course! She had to seize every opportunity, assert herself, become again the enterprising woman who knew how to say yes and no, who chose her path. This dance would be a first decision of her life as a free woman. It was audacious to stay for a moment in the arms of a man other than her own on the dance floor. Daniel Sahel was jealous of the way the young man held her close to him, to lift her up, to put her down with all delicacy. He went to the dance floor, grabbed Ellen by the waist.

"Sir! It's my turn, I have to finish this dance with my wife now!"

He trained her for a few minutes, tired they came to sit down. The evening was a success, Ellen could say that she existed, that she lived, that she was happy. Certainly, her mentality had changed, could she change those around her, who still lived in the past, full of prejudices? Could she make her environment understand that everyone had the right to live their lives without forcing others to follow?

Another battle appeared on the horizon, that of convincing her children. She knew them well. Her idea was to make them accomplices in their newfound happiness. Will she succeed? Her birthday was fast approaching; it was time to reveal her penchant for the old Negro. Confronting her eldest son, sharing with him the love that filled her. She knew his reaction; she gave herself the right to lead her life as she wished. No one could take this love out of her path, this love that guided her to a better life. To oppose this would be tantamount to her funeral, to burying her alive.

She sharpened her words, prepared her lines. The next day, her eldest son Alain invited her to dinner in a Greek restaurant at the United Nations. As usual, he talked to him about his wife, his children, his work. That day, she showed an extraordinary enthusiasm. She listened to him; she had the joy of seeing him.

"I'm happy, Mom! I have everything I need to be happy."

Could it be a coincidence or a thought that could allow his mother to enter into a conversation where he didn't know the outcome? Ellen was relaxed. Her broad smile is to share her son's happiness, but rather a prelude to what she would have spat in the plate.

"Alain, I am overjoyed to see you so happy! Tell me, what am I missing to be as happy as you are? I love you all, you are my children, my grandchildren, my life."

The question was hard for him, he was juggling with words without really answering them. He never imagined for a second that his mother could rebuild his life, modest though it was, after several years of servitude, as Catherine suggested. He emptied his glass of wine and refilled it, looked around, gave the impression of waiting for an answer from somewhere else, then decided to slip in a word that he didn't know how his mother would perceive it.

"You raised us alone, you gave us love, you made us responsible men and women. I wish God would give you everything you need to be as happy as I am."

Alain opened the door, and Ellen was the only one left to enter. She knew her son's temperament well. To rush him in his statement would have been catastrophic; she was looking for the right words, words that would go in the direction of her wish for happiness. In a sung voice, she declared:

"Alain, I'm in love." He jumped on his chair, she held him back. "Since each one of you has his home, I have felt alone and unhappy. I know how difficult it is for you to accept that I have another man in my life other than your father. But at your age, you have to accept my choice, no matter what it is. I need your help, all your support."

"Okay! Mom, you win. However, he shouldn't have to live under your roof! What is he like? Is he small? Is he tall? Is he as handsome as me?" (laughing)

"He is handsome, tall, has an athletic body. He's 68 years old, we give him 40, he's a black man, a black African, I have to introduce him."

Alain became pale, he swallowed his mouth. This unexpected shock made him blush. A glass of water brought down the piece of food that was choking him. With his eyes out of his sockets, he replied to his mother.

"Mommy! Anyone, please, not a nigger! Phew! If he hadn't already done so, Dad would be turning over in his grave!"

"What do you have against black people? They have the same color of blood running through your veins. If it wasn't him, it could have been a Hindi or a Latino. I find them very well educated!"

"Why not Quebecers, French, Italians or English? You've been looking for the chief mendigot!"

Angry, Alain came out of the restaurant, everything was blurring in front of him. He walked away, far from there; he realized that he had forgotten to take his car parked in the alley. Alone in front of her destiny, Ellen let herself wander in bitterness. There was a time when children religiously obeyed their parents, never such a scandal would ever occur in her youth. Desolation darkened her, her soul in disarray, she had collapsed on the table. In panic, the lady on duty ran out. She saw Alain, he was coming back to take his car.

"Sir! Mister! Your mother is dying."

With a giant leap, Alain ran to join his mother. He lifted her up and started shouting, "Call an ambulance!" He felt a terrible shock that made him think. *Was it an act of bravery or an act of cowardice? He blamed himself for having caused his mother discomfort, he congratulated himself for having saved her from certain death. This accident also led Alain to look at the human race in a different light. What was difficult was the marginalization of the black race, of immigrants in front of his children. He compared them to the predatory wild beasts that invade his natural habitat, the United Nations. He did not mince his words when they crossed West Jean-Talon Street. What will he tell his children? That they have magically become honorable citizens again, enjoying the same rights and privileges as him again?*

In spite of all these thoughts, he had not envisaged how the first meeting with this man for whom his mother had become ill would take place. On Sunday morning, at the Montreal General Hospital, Ellen woke up painfully surrounded by her entire family. Flowers here, flowers there, the nurse couldn't figure out where to put them. She heard the word, "Mommy I love you," from her children's mouths, followed by interminable kisses, she looked radiant even though her heart was outside this place. Inside, she was thinking about the future. That of making the man of her choice accepted. Her worries were extinguished like a flame when, in an elegant way. Alain brought Daniel Sahel into the room. The death regained its strength, a cry of joy was heard.

The big question remained for the grandchildren, who is this black man, who spared no one with his pretty words? An answer that only Ellen would give. Back in her home, she embraced her children, she asked for forgiveness for Daniel Sahel. A man she fell in love with, a man with whom she rediscovered life, the only man who had delicately awakened her heart, the only man who could take away her worries, who could transport her beyond passion.

She had a surprise visit; it was her friend Cathy. Cathy was the only woman who didn't like Ellen's new life. She wanted them to stay together as they had been before. Discreetly, she conspired to harm the old nigger. When Alain said goodbye to his mother, Cathy followed him.

"Alain! Alain! Tell me, did Ellen fall as a teenager?" He turned around and stopped walking.

"She is in love, can't you tell?"

"In love with an old nigger, we must do it, eh! What will the neighborhood say? You, who are so famous? And we'll hear everywhere that your mother gets fucked by a nigger? Oh, my God! Save me! What a shame?"

"Mind your own business, you, old bitch!"

"Oh! The bitch is the one who lets the nigger fuck her."

Alain walked toward Cathy with his fist up in the air, she ran away like lightning into his house. He knocked on the door in vain.

"If you don't open this door for me, I'm going to break it down!"

He was going to look out the window like a wolf, wanting to devour the little pig. Cathy made no noise, she remained silent until Alain left. He didn't let go; he came back to open the door with a kick. He dragged her out of bed.

"Listen to me, old fool, if you say a single word about my mother or her unemployment, I'll gouge your eyes out! I'll cut out your tongue!"

"Let go of me! Help, he's going to kill me!"

"Shut the fuck up!"

"Yes! Yes! I'll shut up; I'll shut my mouth, you'll give up killing me, right?"

Alain let go of old Cathy, she was rolling on the bed with her head under her pillow, she started to cry, "I'm not loved by anyone, my own friend abandoned me for a man, my neighbors think I'm crazy, and you want to take my life."

Alain left angry again, he would have avoided this if Cathy had kept her viper's tongue.

Daniel Sahel, the nigger king of the United Nations, as his friends liked to call him, was a man inhabited by desires. As soon as he returned to Ellen's house, he threw himself into her arms, kissed her tenderly and said:

"I'm crazy for you! I will never leave you."

She went away for a moment while she answered the phone, then she came back to jump on him, kissing him.

"I promised myself a thousand and one pleasures when you come back."

Ellen transformed this return to the frolics of the flesh. She had been deprived of it for years, she gave the impression of wanting to make up for lost time, by launching herself into a dizzy spell in her arms, between her legs. A great pleasure poured over her, like a spring invading her veins, her heart, her whole body. Nailed on him by this immense love, she stuck to him, their bodies became one. When they returned to their routine, they congratulated each other, each one boasted that they had taken the best out of both of them. Daniel wanted to formalize this love already known by Ellen's immediate family. He was thinking of his little sister Annie; she knew nothing about her brother who was discreetly living his love relationship. It was about time she knew, that she shared this sudden joy he would say of the man who seemed to feed only on wisdom and advice to others. He turned to the woman in his heart and spoke in a tone full of tenderness.

"Ellen! You didn't know my little sister."

"You didn't introduce me to her, I thought you were alone in this world, alone like me, trying to heal her emotional wounds. What is she like? Little? Tall? Fat or skinny?"

"She's thin and athletic, her name is Annie Sahel. She is the pearl of Africa."

"All men must turn to look at her."

"Oh! Men tear each other apart when she passes in the street, you know, everyone tries to get her attention in his own way."

"I would like to see her."

"For that I have to prepare the ground. I have a hunch that you will get along wonderfully. She has a boy, little Abraham."

"Is she married? Such a beauty cannot stay single for long."

"Hum! She is divorced. My sister is a difficult woman, very hard for her and very hard for men. Her husband had to be as perfect as the sky, the slightest imperfection could cause an uninterrupted duel. The only man capable of containing her is my nephew, Abraham. He is a crooked boy; you will love him too. Abraham is a true Quebecer. Very different from us by his spoken language, he finds fault with all my friends. He is against tobacco, alcohol, drugs and anything that can make people crazy or sick. I have placed a lot of hope in him, I want him to succeed everywhere where I have failed. I want him to be a symbol of family in Canada. I see in him a very great politician, a man of the people, a statesman."

When Annie picked up the phone in the afternoon, she didn't expect to speak to her brother. Usually, he would only call her on Friday night to order his beef feet dish. She was scared for a moment, thinking he was in trouble. The worry betrayed her voice.

"My little sister, excuse me, but you don't look well!"

"I'm fine, thank God. You scared me…are you okay?"

"As if on wheels, I have a surprise for you. I would like to introduce you to the most beautiful woman in the United Nations!"

Annie remained speechless, she thought what joke was he was up to this time, he who confided in no one about his love affairs, how he had gotten to this stage of disclosures.

"A woman from the United Nations, you want to tell me that you have found true love. It must be a rare pearl."

"She is!"

"Don't lose your head so soon!"

"It's official; everyone knows it. I want to tell you before you hear it from another mouth."

"You said everyone knows it."

"Finally, it's a way of marking my words."

"Hum."

She took a long breath. Annie just couldn't believe her ears when she heard her brother whose heart was deeply imbued with love like a stain on a white dress. With her hands on her head, she seemed paralyzed, this little five-letter word sounded like a bomb.

"What an adventure you let yourself get caught up in! A woman at your age is too much trouble, don't you think?"

"You talk too much! I'll be right there."

"All alone?"

"With Ellen!"

"Now, you surprise me. Give me at least half an hour, I have to pick up the house."

"We'll close our eyes; we'll only open it to see you and talk to you."

"Stop it! Will you?"

Shortly after he hung up the phone, a cab stopped in front of the building where Annie lived. Daniel got out first, helping Ellen. He was holding the door.

"That's where she lives."

"It's from Nun's Island."

"She is a nurse; she can afford it."

Annie went through her apartment with a fine-toothed comb, she dusted, she vacuumed the carpet, cleaned the bathroom. As soon as she heard the doorbell ring, she rushed to open it. She displayed a radiant smile of welcome, she gave a hug to the one she was to call sister-in-law, she offered her a bouquet of flowers. She observed her from head to toe, one could see in her eyes an affection for this lady that she had not known until today. She found her extraordinarily young, more beautiful than she had thought. Happiness abounded in Daniel's face.

"Annie, this is the most beautiful woman in the United Nations. Ellen, this is my little sister, Annie."

"You picked the rare flower, Dan!"

"Did I?"

"Yes, she's beautiful!"

Flattered, she didn't expect such a nice welcome. Very quickly, she confided in Annie, she told her about her life before.

"Your brother is a lifesaver for me; he pulled me out of the loneliness that was devouring me, he gave me love, the joy of living a healthy life."

"He had kept himself from telling me anything until today."

"For that, he must go to confession!"

Daniel protested.

"It is out of the question that I confess, I don't know who is behind the curtain. It could be a pedophile, I've read a lot about it in the newspapers, I'd heard about it on the news on the radio."

The bell rang again, it was Abraham. He was coming back from the library with his hands full of books. He didn't expect his uncle to open it for him.

"Hello, my boy!"

Abraham was worried about his mother, so he dropped his burden.

"What happened to Mom? Why are you here?"

"Come on! Pick up your books, we paid you a surprise visit."

"I don't want to see your friends here!"

"Quiet! She's a friend, actually…your future aunt."

He was making his way through, when he was inside, the surprise was total.

"Who is she?" He asked his mother.

"Ellen! Call her Aunt Ellen, she's your uncle's wife-to-be."

"Does he still have the strength to live as a couple? I thought he was finished."

Daniel did the simulated fight against four opponents. When he finished, he was applauded by Ellen and Annie.

"It's called poomséa, my boy."

Abraham fell under the spell of his old uncle. Finally, something unites them. He would like to learn this martial art.

"You amazed me, uncle. I have to go to this school!"

Annie stopped her son Abraham's hobby; what mattered to her was how it was taking her brother to meet

Ellen. She doubted that he was so bold as to approach a woman, and make her a dear friend.

"Say! Which one of you had the initiative to approach the other? And under what circumstances?"

This eloquent question took Daniel Sahel back to the old days, the time when he met Ellen's late husband, the time when he lived just across the street from Ellen's residence. She was a woman of divine beauty who left no one indifferent. No male could resist her charm. All of them followed her with their eyes, when she disappeared from sight, they felt pain in their pants. She was the focal point, the friends offered glasses of beer to her husband to get closer and admire her busts. Others befriended their wives in order to make her the delight of her husband. Daniel thought for a few minutes, he had to digest his dish, take his sacred cup of tea, eat his dessert, in order to better dig into his brain, to make the past appear, a past that seemed to be sealed, inaccessible. Daniel asked for and obtained a second cup of tea, this time, the vault of his memory seemed open, he took advantage of it, he walked in. No sooner had he opened his mouth than he picked up four sugar cubes and dipped them in his tea while Annie looked on with disapproval, a health reason being necessary. Daniel Sahel tasted his tea, once his throat was lubricated with sugar, he decided to go straight to the point.

"I can't talk about my meeting with Ellen without mentioning it to her late husband. He was fortunate among the men who desired her, providence made him pass the moment the sky opened and brought down this rare pearl without escort. He took her and made her his wife. Even the

Greek Goddess of Love, questioned her beauty in front of Ellen."

Embarrassed, Ellen opened a parenthesis.

"I am not as beautiful as the Greek Goddess of Love."

"Yes, you are!" Daniel said. "In all the evenings at the United Nations, you turned away from all the men, the women were jealous to see their husbands succumbing at your feet without getting up. They were bewitched; they saw their wives only through your image."

Annie wanted him to tell his story in a straightforward way. It was difficult for Daniel to get there without evoking the history.

"You talk too much without telling me how you met Ellen, tell me about this third type of encounter."

"Who is the third type?"

"It's you, of course!"

"Well done! You succeeded in demobilizing me, but I won't recapitulate. Let's go as you wanted. Once she was a widow, I followed her everywhere, I was a follower of the church where she went every Sunday. I offered my services to the parish priest so that I could admire her better and get closer to her."

As a good Christian, Annie got carried away.

"You bastard! You enter the church with the idea in mind of courting women instead of praying to God!"

"Not so fast my little sister, I was serving mass too! Although…my attention was directed toward Ellen…and after all, she was a star that came down from the sky…Like all the men I've related, my weakness was grandiose. I was taking pains to reach my goal. Occasionally, I used an old friend to help me. After mass, Ellen was the first to wait in line for confession. I slipped in and entered without being seen and questioning her.

'I listen to you, my daughter, have you sinned?'

'Yes, my father!'

'Which is your sin, my daughter?'

'I feel lonely and I dream to live again a life as a couple with a man.'

'Have you found that man?'

'No, my father, but…I'm ready to accept a man of any nationality who will want me to be my father.'

'Would you accept a black man, my daughter?'

'Yes, my father!'

'You swore fidelity to your late husband…but God is merciful…go, mate as soon as possible…I forgive you my daughter.'"

Annie didn't wait until the end to condemn his brother.

"You took the place of a priest to exploit the misfortunes of poor women, but that's it, you're going straight to hell."

"Let him finish, I think it's very funny!" Ellen added. She had just saved her friend from the claws of his little sister whom he nicknamed the tigress.

"When I had finished, I ran out, afraid that she would fall into the arms of the first black man she would meet along the way. I lost my cane in the rush and by a miracle I found the strength to keep walking. From afar, I could see her turning the corner, I had taken a cab to go down a little closer to her.

'Hello divine beauty! It's me, Daniel Sahel, your former neighbor.'

'Hello, Daniel.'

'As it is fine today, the Lord rewards us after three days of rain, at the end the sun shines for us.'

'Yes, the Lord has always done only good things.'

'No doubt! I would like if…'

'Pardon! I did not understand.'

'I invite you tonight to dinner at a restaurant of your choice to make the most of this beautiful day.'"

Ellen kept silent; he was afraid the answer would be no. But suddenly, he started screaming like crazy in the street when she accepted his invitation. Daniel counted the hours, the minutes, the seconds. Usually, he would complain that the sun disappeared very early, but that day, if he could, he would bring it forward to sunset.

The long-awaited hour arrived; he chartered a cab that took them to the Greek restaurant in the neighborhood on the rue Jean-Talon. He did things in a big way. Table d'hôte reserved with service VIP champagne served at their entrance; an evening worthy of kings and queens.

Ellen did not suspect the reasons for the invitation, she was certain that his prayers had brought him passionate dividends, although she was not sure of the turn of this adventure in which she immersed herself. Daniel Sahel raised his glass to Ellen's health, and once the glasses of champagne crossed each other in reasoning, after a few sips, he magically took out of his pocket a wedding ring adorned with artificial diamonds. He knelt down in front of her and addressed her with words:

"Ellen! With this modest gift, I want us to be friends, I want you to accept it, to wear it on your finger in the name of friendship. This comes from all my soul that shakes for you, your presence alone brings out the joy of living, of hoping, of going beyond the limits where I am supposed to stop. What can I say about the strength of your imposing beauty, which is a source of fulfillment for me?"

Ellen presented her left hand followed by an affectionate smile. She thought she was dreaming, how things could happen as quickly as she had hoped. Was this a miracle. None of her wishes had come true as quickly as this one. Outdated, she abandoned her fate to the Greek Gods. Daniel Sahel shouted victory when his lips touched Ellen's for the first time. He had a hot flush, a great energy that would have energized him. He went around the room announcing to anyone who wanted to hear his exploits.

"Madam, sir, you see the pretty lady sitting at the back of the room? It is me she loves."

At the fourth table, a group of people walked him home, a woman took him by the shoulder and congratulated Ellen. Before they left the restaurant, Ellen's mind was clouded with questions. How could she tell her children, her only friend and neighbor Catherine, about her love? She was worried about the reactions of the people she knew. Ellen expressed her feelings about her immediate environment in this way.

"I'm happy to be by your side, I didn't doubt for a second that you love me…I love you too, I accept this love (they kissed), but there are things that haunt me. How can I announce this happiness that fills me with joy to my family and friends? Help me to find the right words to say it."

"Of course, you can! We can keep it a secret, after all it's just between the two of us. No one should interfere in our relationship, not even the Pope. I propose that we see each other discreetly until the right moment to announce the good news to everyone."

"When will we see again, my great love?"

He waited all evening for this, short sentence gave him back his confidence, the certainty that he had just entered into a loving relationship with the woman whom the men of the United Nations had once coveted. Daniel bent his chest; he called the service staff. He ordered another bottle of champagne. He gazed at Ellen, stretching out his hands and giving her fingertip caresses.

"Tomorrow night at any time. I belong to you, I am at your disposal, my sweet Ellen."

He kissed her hands, he didn't want time to pass, the slightest second counted for this moment of seduction. He apologized for not having put his plan into action in time; if he could he would go back in time to when he was satisfied just by watching her pass in front of him.

The champagne was refilled and the woman on duty brought a large bouquet of the flowers he ordered for the occasion. Ellen was overjoyed and elated with passionate excitement.

"This is the most beautiful bouquet of flowers I have ever received in thirty-five years." She stood up and cried in his arms.

"Stop crying, it's never too late, you see, we are celebrating a unique event, a union for better and for worse, even though we are not married. By the way, marriage is just a formality, a way to show your love in front of family and friends."

"Absolutely! We don't ask permission from others to love each other, to live together."

Daniel in turn rejoiced to see everything bathed in oil.

"These words drive me crazy! Of course, crazy about you, Ellen. I still haven't gotten over my emotions of seeing you sitting at the table next to me, telling me that you love me. No, I am not dreaming…I am living my dreams, the door to Eden is wide open to me. I enter as a king at heart in search of his queen, a queen sitting on his throne, sending me signals of love."

When he finished summing up his young adventure, Abraham was dozing on the couch next to his mother.

"This is a story worthy of a novel," said Annie. "You hid your affection for her from me, no words escaped your lips, no signs to tell me you are in love. I raise my hat to both of you and I am sure you will lead a happy life. And now that we're here, when is the wedding?"

"My little sister, everything comes to those who know how to wait."

That was how Daniel Sahel introduced Ellen to his family. He responded to Ellen's slightest whim by returning her idol, an icon, a good-luck charm.

To celebrate Julien's thirty-fifth birthday, Alain rented a cottage in the Laurentians, a picturesque spot, ideal as a family meeting place. The chalet was built on the side of a mountain that looked like a bird's nest perched on the hillside, surrounded by trees and a clear lake. For this occasion, Ellen invited Annie and Abraham. Two days earlier, she had visited the site with her daughter-in-law, her grandchildren, and Daniel Sahel.

After the preparations were completed, they waited for Julien's arrival with Alain. When he learned that the old Negro, the family's host, was none other than his mother's lover, Julien saw his world crumble. The news sounded to his ears like a bomb, destroying all his childhood memories that he shared a thousand and one times with his father. He anticipated the future with bitterness. *What strength would have brought his gentle mother back so low? And this man, this old nigger, where did he come from? How had he entered his mother's life?* These were questions he would like to have answered. Along the way, he had quite an argument about it, he agreed not to believe it.

"Alain, how did you let Mom deteriorate so badly?"

"What could you do better if you were there?"

"Make me feel guilty, I'm away at school."

"And you're insinuating that you'll do better than me?…Down! Let her live, is there a reason that we are happy and she is not? Diversity in the family will give us spice, don't you think?"

"Listen, Alain, she gave her word of honor that she would not remarry!"

"Yes, but only crazy people don't change their minds, are you going to blame her for that? She has given us everything up to today, she has made us men capable of navigating in this tumultuous society. It is now up to us to support her in her choice."

"Are you talking about intention or choice?"

"Open your ears well, listen to me! Her choice is made, she is in love. I had your reaction; I made her sick when I left the restaurant. She had been sick, and I made her sick by my behavior toward her. Is that enough for you?"

"Is this a joke? You want me to believe that she lives with a black man? A nigger? Do you see me calling a nigger my uncle? What a shame? This relationship must be undone immediately."

Alain got carried away:

"If you're going away to give Mommy a heart attack, it's best to go back to where you came from!"

"By the way, my birthday doesn't matter to you, it's the event of the old nigger and widow you're celebrating!"

Alain calmed his brother, Julien, promising to contain his anger, but he was afraid of exploding when the time came to shake hands with Daniel Sahel. As soon as he arrived, the whole family stood at the door, singing the famous song *bonne faith*, everyone made his wishes. Julien looked down in front of these manifestations of pleasure. Alain was expecting it, he sank into deep thought. We saw him stingy with words, he was going around in circles, unable to sit down. He was fleeing from this place that had become unbearable, his mind was elsewhere. He saw again his youth, the tenderness he received from his father and his mother, the joy of life, the pleasure of receiving everything without sharing, the selfishness of thinking only of himself in all circumstances.

Julien had sweat on his forehead. It was as if a gigantic volcano was erupting, invading his whole body. He was in denial, he lost reality, he wanted things to happen according to his taste, his desires. This time, he resisted his every whim, that of seeing Daniel Sahel's departure from the chalet. Dissatisfaction strangled him; he walked out the front door, stepped backward with his hands folded, looking up at the cloudy sky. He would like to be like one of those birds perched in the corpses, singing in turn. He envied the squirrels with their tails up in the air, chasing each other, jumping from one tree branch to the next without worrying about predators. When he lowered his eyes, it was to keep his distance from a skunk looking for meal in the garbage around the house. This behavior worried Ellen, what's wrong with it! What should she do to make him smile again? She didn't know the real reason; she didn't think for a second that the old Negro she was in love with was the cause.

The heaviness of the atmosphere in the chalet also worried Daniel Sahel. He would like that Ellen would be sitting in front of him, look up and tell him that everything will be all right. He hoped that Julien would find in him a man he could trust, a friend, a person he could confide in. All his hope vanished when he saw him enter the room with his head down. Against all odds, Julien asked for and obtained a short walk in the company of his host, who rushed outside, displaying a radiant smile. He sincerely believed that the game was won, everything had just returned to normal. They walked along the path that led to the top of the mountain. There, a panoramic view awaited Daniel Sahel. He breathed his lungs full of oxygen, he had a euphoric effect.

"Ah, how wonderful, thank you for showing me all these natural treasures. The only Laurentians I know is the one I used to sit at the table with my friends, I mean the beer."

"I'm not in the mood for jokes."

"And for what? Life is beautiful! All life will be affectionate if you smile at the grandiose sky that offers us this beautiful nature. I know what's bothering you, you hate seeing me next to your mother, don't you really?"

Julien was relieved to have indirectly dragged him to work. He went on the offensive.

"Good deduction! Go on, you're not far from my vision."

"What will I do to make you and me friends?"

"If I answer this question, will you respect my will?"

"In part, depending on your demands."

"You see, you're leaving yourself some leeway."

"You don't teach the old monkey how to make a face."

"Let's get straight to the point, how did you know my mother?"

"Am I supposed to tell you?"

"Of course! A good mother of a family, a midwife suddenly breaks with all her beliefs and falls in love in the arms of a puppet, a nigger, a human waste, there had to be some explanation."

Daniel Sahel nodded his shoulders, confused, he had not wanted to live the intolerable atmosphere. He thought about how to mitigate this unhealthy climate that could cause damage. As a wise old man, he had a little smile on his lips and then let go of the piece that made his interlocutor bold.

"Fate, my son!"

"You insult me on top of that, old toad! You can't reach my father's ankles! I know what you've done, you've bewitched her…voodoo is in your blood!"

Daniel Sahel moderated the tone, he was looking for the words to coax him, to bring him to his senses.

"Listen, my boy!"

Julien got carried away once again, he took him by the shirt, hatred appeared on his face, he shook him violently.

"I forbid you to call me my boy residue!"

Daniel had the impression that the young people had given themselves words to attack only him. His wish was to see Julien let go of his shirt without using force.

"Gentleman, I know that kindness outweighs your anger, calm down."

"You talk too much! You don't make me angry! Look me in the eyes, your life is not worth the life of raccoons or rabbits."

"What do you want to do to me? Kill me? Kill me and that's the end of it."

"Once again, shut your filthy mouth!"

"No! Not so fast! Let's go back to your mother, this beautiful woman, this elegant lady I offer her my heart and soul. She is entitled to the freedom to love, to blossom. Now, I am the happy to be the chosen one, the man of her life, I feel in me a boldness that overflows despite my age. I am able to defend it even against an army. I've let you get on your horses enough, get down on the ground now, you poor little bastard!"

"Now you've crossed the line. One more word and you'll find yourself in pieces at the bottom of the cliff!"

Convinced that diplomacy had inflated the head of his young jailer, he gave way to a passive but provocative offensive.

"I see your feet are shaking, you're peeing in your pants. Imagine that I've already faced tougher ones than you think."

Julien let go of Daniel, he moved backward, then came punched him on the stomach. Daniel burst out laughing, this laughter increased his anger by one notch. Julian came back again in force to hit him, when he had not succeeded, he seized a dead tree branch, he advanced toward him.

"This time, say your prayer, the wolves won't even eat your rotten flesh, I'll send them away for the worms."

Daniel Sahel found the threat of his little warrior amusing; he saw through his little head a spoiled child, badly fed, who thought he was a dungeon.

"Listen, little fool! Drop that stick before I beat your ass!"

Julien ran for the third time in the direction of Daniel, he hit left and right, he turned around, he could no longer see his adversary. Out of nowhere, Daniel shouted a dreadful cry. He made a spiral jump, his feet were to slap Julien in the face, causing him to fall. Laying on the ground, his head resting on the piece of dry tree branch that was his weapon, Julien was woken up by Daniel Sahel. He opened one eye and then closed it again. He had not understood how he had found himself in this position. Unconscious, he was unable to assess how long his ordeal had lasted. Five minutes? Fifteen minutes? He still abandoned himself on the ground, he was living the cruel experience he thought was reserved for his host. The true warrior was the one who had the audacity to help his adversary without reducing him to ashes.

Daniel had the impression that an immense pressure weighed on his chest, he would have to take the spoiled baby back to the chalet. The second attempt was the right one, Julien raised his head once again, he moaned in pain. For a moment, he thought he was dying. When he came to, he hadn't believed that this frail old man would have such strength to send him to the mat. He believed that he was endowed with an occult force. Standing, he walked slowly down to the river, taking water in the palms of his hands to sprinkle himself. Julien was washing and washing his face, he noticed that he had a bump on his forehead, a scratch on his knees. The tension had collapsed out of him, he took a deep breath to ease his pain.

"In the name of God, where did you learn to defend yourself like that?"

"My grandfather always told me: 'Never show your strength to your enemy, it will take away the surprise in battle'."

"But I am not your enemy!"

"Yes, you are! You were just now."

"In fact, I won't have anything gained by annoying you."

"That doesn't prevent you from getting a beating, on everything when you have a big mouth. My grandfather also used to say: 'If a young Poulin wants to eat the grass on your land, you have to put an apple in his throat'."

"What does all this bullshit mean, you didn't answer my question?"

"Yes, I answered your question, try to understand the meaning of my grandfather's words, they have virtues that can serve as a guide in the future."

Arriving at the chalet, to Daniel Sahel's astonishment, Julien invented a whole story to explain his fall. The old nigger nodded his head, not wanting to upset his young companion. Cohabitation in the chalet was difficult as time went by. Abraham had known his sad days, he who, unwaveringly facing alone at the United Nations, the friends of his uncle gathered in their eternal discussions of system that made them outcasts, parasites, men without work, worthless, eaten away by loneliness, regrets for having abandoned everything in their countries, their best living conditions, their honors, their notoriety.

He looked up at his mother, he thought that despite all that she was shouting, he had a background of truth. What was he going to defend in the future? The immigrant he once called a parasite or the system into which he was born? He also thought of his friend Karim whose parents had packed up after the failure of Eldorado, after they were forced to return because the mentality in their native country had changed, they were lost again. Unable to regain their place in society, they were forced to retrace their steps, to go where they thought they would find the best life they dreamed of. Abraham thought that, in fact, they were as bad as the homeless. They really had no country; they were not happy anywhere.

This was the first time he considered what would happen to him, would he inherit the hardship of all these immigrants from all over the world landing in the Promised Land?

Annie watched her son for long time, she knew something was working on him. She was going to talk to him.

"And then, did you like the countryside?"

The long silence that Abraham kept made him say that he was not happy, he whispered in her ear, "They are racist, these children! They speak badly of us, let's go mother!"

Annie rejoiced that she was always right when she told Abraham that he would never be a full citizen in the eyes of all of them. But she didn't come to disturb the party; she couldn't talk too much about discrimination in an already plausible atmosphere.

Abraham would not have been himself, overwhelmed by emotions he wondered who he was *A Quebecer? An immigrant? Yet none of his white friends spoke that language. Was it out of politeness? He who did not hesitate to go to war against his own, who disowned them, who treated them badly, who disrespected them, could not imagine that he would be served this medicine, that he would be politely told to leave, that he was different from this world where he would go? His place of birth was here.*

It was feeding time; Daniel Sahel was warming the raised oxen's feet that Annie brought him. He poured the contents of the pot into a large dish that he put on the table, he took care to slip a note for the children to avoid eating this exotic dish. In a bottle used for canning, there was a spicy sauce that he nicknamed atomic bomb. Daniel challenged anyone who ate a teaspoon of this hot pepper to win a nice twenty dollars; if he couldn't swallow it, he had to wash all the dishes. Many decided to take up the challenge, while the men were arguing over who would start first, the women were already at the table. Suddenly, a cry of distress was heard. With a tight throat, Simone's discolored face hurt to breathe for a few seconds. She thought she was dying. She drank several glasses of water; she could not open her eyes.

"Milk! Give her milk!" Daniel Sahel screamed at the top of his lungs.

Annie ran to get a jug from the fridge, she poured a large quantity of milk into a bowl, any container she could get her hands on. As soon as she drank, Simone filled up like a newborn baby. Annie persisted, she managed to make her swallow a small amount. Here, she was breathing at full lungs.

She didn't understand how humans like her could resist such chili-pepper capable of making her die? But by the way, it all boiled down to customs, according to Daniel Sahel, this pepper was part of African legend; it had an aphrodisiac virtue on everything for men in search of supreme virility. A calm reigned in the room, the little children began to get angry, many did not believe and wanted to try some. Go play outside! One of the adults shouted angrily before grabbing the legendary dish under the astonishing gaze of the women who were already preparing glasses of milk as a first treatment.

The men who were arguing over the primacy of tasting the chili miracle began to desist one after the other, Daniel took a spoonful and swallowed it without the slightest shock.

"You see? In my country, we recognize men by their endurance to all things."

There was silence in the dining room, Ellen kissed her man, hugged him and agreed with him.

Plates in hand, they paraded around the table to help themselves. Among all the dishes present, ox feet were the choice of several, he was given notes ranging from twenty to thirty out of ten, they asked for the recipe.

The next day, Catherine found it curious that her best gossip, being absent, wanted her right after mass. She went to the door and rang the bell. She left and came back again. Ellen opened the door.

"Where were you? The whole town was looking for you."

"And why was that? Would anyone have thought I'd vanished off the face of the earth?"

"You didn't tell me, worried I alerted your children."

"Are you crazy?"

Ellen picked up the phone, assuring her children that she was home. Catherine snooped around, and noticed the bouquet of flowers in a large decorated pot from Greece on the corner of the living room. She racked her brains, wondering when the florist would deliver the flowers and when Ellen would receive such a large bouquet. She wanted to be clear-headed.

"Ellen! You're being secretive!"

"Sneaky, about what?"

"Where did you get this bouquet of flowers? Did someone give it to you? Or did you pick it up at the cemetery?"

"Poor bitch! Do you see me stealing flowers from the dead? I'm a living person, I have to enjoy life as it should be before I die."

"Ah! You're talking like a teenage girl who's just met her first love."

"Am I supposed to tell you everything?"

"I think so, I tell you everything; you know everything about me, you know my intimate secrets."

"That you were making up so that I would spill mine on you, right?"

"Let's forget the bouquet of flowers, shall we go to bingo tonight?"

"My kids will pick me up, you go by yourself."

"Good! I won't waste time, bye!"

Catherine put on her clothes; she went out to wait for the bus for bingo. Meanwhile at the United Nations, for the first time, the comrades were sweating the adventures of the man they preferred to call the Dean. Although Daniel didn't have a brilliant career in engineering, he was successful with the ladies of his generation. Finally, the news of his work as a janitor was overshadowed by the arrival of Samuel on the scene.

Sam was a young married man with two children. His job as a traveling salesman brought him only a few meager dollars a month. He endured these conditions by braving all winter, summer, fall and spring temperatures. As a vacuum cleaner salesman, he was ringing thousands of doorbells a day, and at each stop he had to convince customers to lean for his product. A hard work, it happened months that he sold nothing. Dragging a heavy luggage on his back made him bend his back. Once a jealous man, when he arrived from work, threw his promotional material out of the window and pushed him down the stairs. Sam found himself on the second floor below, his knees were skinned. The sprained right ankle was keeping him at home without resources. Sam couldn't stand to hear his children starve, too proud to apply for social assistance, he was begging his former telemarketing boss to allow him to return to his old job. This time, he had to sell a weekly magazine. The first call took him back in time, when companies turned a deaf ear to his university education in Beirut. The instinct to survive the difficult times had hardened him, and he refused to give up. His motto was to take whatever luck offered him, however small.

His first call reminded him of the efforts he had made at another time, in that small, partitioned office with a telephone and a detailed list of contact information for potential clients. A lady who had managed to put her little girl to sleep with pain and misery wiped her anger away when she picked up the call. "You woke up my child! Would you come back in and making her sleep?" She hung up the line. Sam felt guilty, thinking about his children who just now had sunken bellies. If he could, he would go and apologize to this lady. The second call came from a sports hockey fan, absorbed in the Montreal Canadiens game against the Boston team, and the man poured his anger on him. "Here's another one of those Ostie des Tabarnaques! I'm listening to my game, do you understand now! Don't call here again Christ!" On the third call, he was called 'shit flies.' Is it too much for a return to telemarketing?

Four hours of work without selling a magazine, four hours spent amortizing insults, enduring anger, he got only his meager basic hourly wage paid by the day.

Realizing that he wouldn't make a fortune under these conditions, he went randomly knocking on the doors of factories. He asked the same question: "Do you have a job for a young immigrant father? I have three mouths to feed." Everywhere else, we would burst out laughing, we would take great joy in ridiculing him. Samuel felt his pressure mounting, so he took a few steps back toward the exit, just long enough to dissipate his anger. "We have nothing for you here," said a little sucker traumatized him at the door of the establishments. The cruel, unhealthy pleasure he had experienced in this last factory, the foreman appeared in the middle of the humiliation, he shouted: "I got a work for you!

Come here, are you able to pack the goods? I mean put them in the boxes?"

It was a melody to his ears. He spent the day of training, listening to the boss's instructions. In a way, he was under the supervision of the workers who made faces at him from time to time. Although he was outraged by this parade of intimidation, he was determined to hold on to this unexpected ephemeral hope.

Samuel told his wife the good news, finally a job he hadn't known how long it would last. He got up with happiness, put on traditional music, and danced around the kitchen table. Sabrina, his wife, did not recognize the man who was on the verge of depression, comforted by a miracle. She, who used to cheer him up at every setback, had a skeptical smile on her face until he brought home a few dollars.

A month of intolerant work every day brought its share of insults, he was amazed to see all these workers, full of hatred, rising up against his presence, throwing residue in his face for no apparent reason. The constant tension overcame his desire to continue his work in the factory. Sabrina probably had a flair for not dancing that morning, in fact, she knew that it would be another job that would end up being a fish job.

The crew handed over an envelope containing a few dollars for Samuel's family.

"Go back to your children! Kiss them for us."

"I don't know how to thank you; I regret having had a fight with the Dean. I wasn't myself; I can't stand it. Often, I didn't know what I was doing."

Daniel Sahel approached him and took him in his arms.

"This sinister affront had turned into happiness for me. I have a beautiful wife at my disposal, and it's a little thanks to you, my little one!" (laughter)

Samuel knew Amir from Lebanon; it was a comfort to him to have surrounded himself with people sharing his sorrows.